NEW WORLD

'I'm helping to test a game — and it's brilliant. I'm even getting paid for doing it . . .'

But are things really that simple?

When Miriam and Stuart step into the shifting, addictive world of virtual reality, every move they make is monitored. Hesketh, who developed the game, is determined that the tests will succeed. So is the games company which has millions invested in the New World project. Miriam and Stuart are the guinea-pigs and, as the game tightens its hold, they become aware that something — or someone — is playing on their deepest, secret fears. Is this part of the tests? Or has someone broken into the game?

Gillian Cross has been writing children's books for over fifteen years. Before that, she took English degrees at Oxford and Sussex Universities, and she has had various jobs including working in a village bakery and being an assistant to a Member of Parliament. She is married with four children and lives in Warwickshire. Her hobbies include orienteering and playing the piano. She won the Carnegie Medal for *Wolf* and the Smarties Prize and the Whitbread Children's Novel Award for *The Great Elephant Chase*.

Other Oxford books by Gillian Cross

The Iron Way
Revolt at Ratcliffe's Rags
A Whisper of Lace
The Dark Behind the Curtain
Born of the Sun
On the Edge
Chartbreak
Roscoe's Leap
A Map of Nowhere
Wolf
The Great Elephant Chase
Pictures in the Dark
Tightrope

For younger readers

The Demon Headmaster
The Prime Minister's Brain
The Revenge of the Demon Headmaster
The Demon Headmaster Strikes Again
The Demon Headmaster Takes Over

NEW WORLD

Gillian Cross

OXFORD
UNIVERSITY PRESS

OXFORD
UNIVERSITY PRESS

Great Clarendon Street, Oxford OX2 6DP

Oxford University Press is a department of the University of Oxford.
It furthers the University's objective of excellence in research, scholarship,
and education by publishing worldwide in

Oxford New York

Athens Auckland Bangkok Bogotá Buenos Aires Calcutta
Cape Town Chennai Dar es Salaam Delhi Florence Hong Kong Istanbul
Karachi Kuala Lumpur Madrid Melbourne Mexico City Mumbai
Nairobi Paris São Paulo Shanghai Singapore Taipei Tokyo Toronto Warsaw

with associated companies in Berlin Ibadan

Oxford is a registered trade mark of Oxford University Press
in the UK and in certain other countries

British Library Cataloguing in Publication Data available

ISBN 0 19 271852 5

1 3 5 7 9 10 8 6 4 2

Printed in Great Britain by
Biddles Ltd, Guildford and King's Lynn

K & K: ELECTRONIC MEMO
HESKETH BARRINGTON TO JOHN SHELLEY
PRIORITY: NORMAL

The test is about to start!

Christine Riley has completed the advance training
and both Subjects are ready. Subject A (the girl) will
come here to play. I'm waiting for her to arrive now.
Subject B (the boy) will play at his own home.

Estimated duration of tests — two months.

Chapter 1

'Two months? You can't be serious! You're going on a computer course for *two months?*'

'It's only three evenings a week,' Miriam muttered. She walked on down the school drive, avoiding Debbie's eyes.

'Oh. Great,' Debbie said sarcastically. 'Only three evenings of boring old computering. You'll have a bit of time left over for me then?'

'Don't be silly.'

Miriam was impatient—but not with Debbie. It was the keeping the secret that annoyed her. Why couldn't she just explain? If Debbie understood what was really going on, she wouldn't be scowling like that. She'd be pleading to join in.

And it would only take a whisper to change her expression. *It's not really a computer course. That's just what they told me to say. What I'm actually doing is helping to test a game—and it's brilliant. I'm even getting paid for doing it. You'll go mad when I tell you . . .*

But she couldn't tell. She'd promised.

Debbie swung her bag sulkily, only just missing Miriam's legs. 'Oh, come on. Give it a miss today. Then we can go down to the Centre, and meet those boys from Asher's.'

'I've got to go. Honestly,' Miriam said.

Debbie swung her bag again, harder. It missed Miriam and hit the bicycle that was swooping past them. The girl on the bike arched one elegant eyebrow, but she didn't say a word. She just put a foot to the ground and pushed off again, into the traffic. Debbie glared after her.

'You're getting like *that*,' she said savagely. 'All brains and no fun. I bet you wish you were still friends with her, don't you?'

'Connie?' Miriam watched the familiar, self-possessed figure on the bicycle as it wove its way up the road. 'I'm nothing like her. She wouldn't go on a computer course. Electronic bugging's more in her line.'

She hadn't meant to sound bitter. Why should she care what Connie was like? It was a long time since they had been friends. But a sharp, sour note crept into her voice, and Debbie nodded gloomily.

'You wait,' she said darkly. 'You'll change.'

'Don't be stupid.' Miriam glanced up the road, to make sure her bus wasn't coming. 'This is only a short course. It's not going to make any difference to me.'

'That's what *you* think!'

Debbie tossed her head and stamped off up the road. For a moment, Miriam was tempted to go after her. To whisper the tiny, crucial hint in her ear and make her smile again. But before she could move, she saw something that stopped her. A bright green estate car, threading its way through the tangled traffic.

Christine Riley's car.

It was like a reminder. Because Christine was the one who had made her make the promise. The very first time they met. *I won't tell anyone. Not until I get permission from K & K. I'll keep everything secret.* Without that promise, Christine would never have let her join in the tests. And she wouldn't have been turning away from Debbie this afternoon and catching the bus to K & K, to meet Christine's boss. Hesketh.

Miriam stared at the car as it crawled into town. That car was part of the whole business. Christine was off to meet the boy — Stuart — and set up the game in his house for him, while Miriam went to K & K. After all the instructions and training and promises, they were starting. It was finally going to happen.

Miriam felt her heart beating faster. Picking up her bag, she turned her back on Debbie and walked slowly to the bus stop, to catch the bus out of town.

She and Stuart were going to meet at last. In the New World.

4

* * *

Three-quarters of an hour later, she was sitting in a big, empty room in K & K, staring across the table at a blank television screen.

'Ready?' called the man at the back of the room.

It was Hesketh. Miriam couldn't see him but, as his fingers rattled on the computer keyboard behind her, she could picture his hunched, heavy shoulders and his crumpled suit.

'Ready,' she said.

The keyboard clacked again, and she leaned forward and stared across the table. The blank monitor opposite was not showing anything yet, except the reflection of her own face, but in a moment it would come to life. She would see Stuart. And on the other monitor, in his house, he would see a face called 'Miriam'. A sharp, clever face, framed by straight black hair.

The screen fizzed and Miriam's heart gave a single, hard thud.

Now.

Her fingers clutched the shiny folder on the table, feeling the embossed, golden letters — *K & K: A Whole New World* — and she gazed at the scrambled white dots that crackled crazily in front of her.

Then the picture cleared. A boy's face stared back at her, blinking slightly, as though his own screen was too bright. Then he beamed, leaning forward eagerly.

Oh dear. Miriam felt a little flicker of disappointment. He was *small.* Thin and keen, with big, moony glasses and a spindly neck. The kind of boy who tried too hard at everything, and stood too close to you.

Remembering that he could see her as well, she smiled cheerfully. 'Hi.'

'Hi!' the boy said. Too loudly. He blinked again.

How old was he? Thirteen? He couldn't be much more. Miriam peered at the books behind his head, trying to pick

5

up some clues about him, but all she saw was an untidy jumble. The shelves were stacked with magazines and old, curling postcards, and a set of headphones dangled from one side.

At the back of the room, Hesketh muttered impatiently. 'Get on with it, you two. Or are you waiting for me to introduce you?'

Miriam shook her head. 'Shall I start?' she said to the screen.

Stuart nodded and leaned further forward.

'OK, then. I'm Miriam Enderby. I'm fourteen, and I'm not at home — you can probably see that. They couldn't put the New World stuff in there, because I live on a boat, so I'm going to play here. I don't know why they want me in the test, because I never play computer games, and — '

'Oh, but they picked you out at random,' Stuart interrupted eagerly. 'There's nothing special about *you*.' Then he heard what he'd said, and went suddenly and startlingly red.

Oh dear, Miriam thought again. But she smiled harder, before he could start to apologize. 'So what about you?'

It was like pulling out a cork. Craning his head at the screen, Stuart suddenly began to talk at top speed. 'I'm Stuart Jones, and I'm fourteen.' (*Fourteen? With a face like that?*) 'I've got two brothers and one sister, and I enjoy inventing gadgets and running my own experiments. I write computer games as well — haven't come up with a winner yet, though — and I've tested dozens of things for K & K, because my dad works in the Marketing Department, but — '

'But you've never played anything like this before!'

That was Hesketh, cutting off the babble of words in mid-stream. He came striding up the room and leaned over Miriam's shoulder, pushing his head close up to hers, to share her camera.

6

'This is the big one,' he said. 'The game that's going to put K & K years ahead of the opposition. So let's get it rolling. Where's Christine?'

'I'm right here,' Christine Riley said. Stuart ducked his head sideways and her face appeared next to his. 'Hallo, Miriam. You found your way all right?'

Miriam nodded. 'Yes, thanks.'

'And how are you getting on with the boss? I told you he was an ogre, didn't I?'

That was almost laughable. Hesketh was big all right, but hardly an ogre. He was crumpled and vague, with a stringy pony-tail straggling down his back and a little gold ear-ring. More funny than frightening. Miriam smiled politely.

'He hasn't eaten me yet.'

Hesketh scowled at the screen. 'I'll eat *you*, Christine, if these two aren't word perfect. Have they got the security rules at their fingertips?'

'Don't panic,' Christine was calm. 'I'm sure they could say them in their sleep.'

Miriam nodded, and Hesketh whipped round to face her.

'All right. Let's hear you, then.'

She began to recite, ticking the points off on her fingers. 'We mustn't tell *anyone* about the tests. Or talk about the equipment. Or about anyone we meet at K & K. We can't contact each other outside the game, and if anyone starts asking questions—'

She was rattling the words off without thinking about them. The rules seemed perfectly reasonable to her, and she assumed they were some kind of standard procedure for games testing at K & K. But suddenly Stuart interrupted her.

'Why not?'

'What?' Miriam stopped, caught off balance, and Hesketh leaned in closer, so that his shoulder brushed against her.

'Why not *what*?'

7

Stuart went red again, but he leaned forward stubbornly. '*Why* can't we contact each other outside the game? You've never said that before. And talking it over with the others is part of the fun.'

'Not this time,' Hesketh murmured. 'This time, it's different. You're testing New World.'

His voice was low, but it wasn't gentle. It lingered on the last two words in a way that made Miriam's scalp prickle.

'There's never been anything like this,' he went on softly. 'If we get it out before the competition can catch up, we'll clean up the market. So there are people out there who'd pay a fortune to find out what we're doing. Or slit throats.'

Miriam swallowed. 'And you're trusting *us?*'

'Some risks have to be taken.' Hesketh looked round at her. His face was very close. She could see the heavy skin of his jaw and the fine, red veins in the whites of his eyes. 'You're old enough to understand how serious we are. If you break the security rules, we shan't treat you like dear little children.'

A long shiver ran up Miriam's back. 'I understand,' she said smoothly. Out of the corner of her eye, she saw Stuart nod, his eyes fixed on Hesketh, as though he were mesmerized.

'OK, then!' Hesketh straightened up, rubbing his hands together. 'Let's have a trial run. Are you all set up at that end, Christine?'

'Set up and ready to switch on.' Christine Riley was just as businesslike as he was, but she spared time for a smile at Stuart and Miriam. 'You two had better take a last look at each other. Next time you meet, you'll be . . . quite different.'

Stuart's eyes gleamed behind the thick, distorting lenses and he raised a hand to wave. 'Great. See you in cyberspace, Miriam!'

'Fine,' Miriam said. She couldn't sound as excited as he did, but she felt her body tensing. Ready to begin.

Then Hesketh walked away from her, towards the back of the room, and she heard the keyboard clatter. Stuart disappeared and the light went out of the screen.

'Ready?' Hesketh said, for the second time.

Miriam gathered her things and stood up. Her reflection slid off the edge of the screen, leaving it a blank, featureless grey. 'Ready.'

Hesketh opened the door and ushered her out, pulling a small plastic card from his inside pocket. Half-way down the corridor, he stopped and swiped the card through a slot in a plain, unlabelled door.

'This is the test room.'

'Where all the equipment is?'

'That's right. I'll come and watch you put it on today. Just to check you remember everything Christine told you.' He pushed the door and stepped back, to let Miriam into the room first.

It was very bare. A small, square space, with a grey carpet and no ordinary furniture. Just a black plastic suitcase on the floor, and a low, black pillar, like the one Christine Riley had brought to show her. The Game Tower.

Hesketh walked across and picked up the case. 'OK. Let's see you do it.'

Miriam looked down at the keyboard on top of the game tower. 'I tell it my name first. Right?'

Hesketh nodded gravely, and she typed in the letters. M-I-R-I-A-M. Then she took the case and flicked the catches open. They glinted silver as she lifted the lid.

'Your explorer's kit,' Hesketh said softly.

Miriam's skin tingled again, and she stared down into the case. All the kit was there, each piece in its own slot. The single glove. The belt. The Game Helmet — like heavy goggles, with earpieces and interwoven straps. And the three clumsy bracelets.

She took the bracelets out first. As she clicked them into place — one round her left wrist and the other two round her ankles — she could almost hear Christine Riley

9

chuckle. *Virtual jewellery they call this. I can't say I care for Hesketh's taste, but they're not meant to look pretty. They help to tell the computer where you are.*

So did the belt. Miriam put that on next, buckling it quickly round her waist. Then she pulled out the glove.

Hesketh didn't move. He hardly blinked. But his eyes followed every movement she made as she slid her fingers into it and wriggled the material over the back of her hand.

The basic glove was light and elastic, but it had stiff ridges along the backs of the fingers, and a thick, heavy wristband. Pulling the ridges straight, Miriam adjusted the wristband until it lay snug and tight against her skin. Then she snapped the fastening shut, remembering Christine's voice again.

There mustn't be anything between your wrist and the glove. No bangles or watches. Not even a shirt sleeve. It's a very important glove, because it's your control. When you want to move more than a step or two, you point. And when you want to pick something up, you grab.

Miriam practised the actions now, grabbing at the air, and then straightening her forefinger to point across the room. The wristband rubbed a little, and she ran a finger underneath the edge, to ease it.

'It has to be a close fit,' Hesketh said quickly. 'Because of the pneumatic sensors. They inflate against your fingers, so you can *feel* the things you touch in the game.'

Why say that? Christine Riley had spelt it out already. Miriam hesitated and looked down at the glove, but Hesketh didn't leave her time for thinking. He pulled the Game Helmet out of the case.

'Better get this on, or Stuart will be way ahead of you. Want me to help?'

'No, thank you.'

Miriam took the helmet and stepped away to settle it on her head, adjusting the straps so that the two little screens sat one in front of each eye. They were dull and empty now, but in a moment they would light up, each one giving her a

10

slightly different picture. Windows on the New World. She shut her eyes and took a deep breath.

'Shall I switch on?'

As if in answer, there was a sudden *beep* from the Game Tower. Hesketh grinned lopsidedly.

'You'd better. Unless you want Stuart to take charge of everything.'

Him? He couldn't take charge of a milk bottle. Miriam reached round to the back of her helmet and grabbed the two sides of the clasp. For an instant she fumbled. Then she found the right slot and pushed the clasp together firmly, until it clicked.

And the screens in front of her eyes blossomed into light.

Chapter 2

Tall, grey stone walls towered in front of her, not as real as a photograph but grimly believable, like a good cartoon. She was standing in a stark, shadowy dungeon, with globs of green slime rolling down the walls, and instruments of torture stacked in one corner. High above her head, a tiny grating let in feeble light and down at the far end she could just make out the huddled white bones of a skeleton.

Very creepy. She looked right, trying to work out what she was meant to do. And as she turned her head, the images in front of her eyes moved too.

But they didn't move quite in time with her body. There was a slight, unpleasant lag. She blinked and stopped, staring at the heavy wooden door on the right hand wall. It had a large keyhole and a little barred opening at head height.

Was she supposed to open it?

Experimentally, she raised her right hand, with the forefinger extended. It appeared in front of her face a split second later as a plain grey shape. It had no lines or nails or knuckles, but it was pointing straight at the door.

And it worked. Immediately, the door seemed to swim nearer, and she realized that she was gliding forward towards it. Lowering her hand, she grabbed at the big black door handle — and under her fingers she felt its solid shape.

It's only the pressure pads inside the glove. An illusion. But it felt real enough. Slowly she turned her hand and pushed at the door.

'It's locked,' said a voice from behind.

Stuart was watching her! Caught off guard, Miriam whirled round, and the room lurched sickeningly. Then it caught up with her, and she found herself gazing at a featureless grey shape, like the silhouette of a corpse. It

12

raised one arm and came gliding over the floor towards her.

'There must be a key somewhere,' it said.

It had no mouth to open and close, but it spoke with Stuart's voice. And it stood too close to her, just as she had known that Stuart would. If they had really been in the same room, she would have felt its breath on her cheek.

She took a step back. 'OK, so there's a key. Where is it, then?'

Stuart turned slowly, scanning the dungeon. He was half-way, looking behind Miriam, when there was a loud scrabbling noise, and she heard him gasp.

'What's the matter?' she said.

Whipping round, she felt her stomach see-saw as the room jerked after her. At the far end of the dungeon was a large rat. It was sitting in the darkest corner, its yellow fangs bared in a snarl and its eyes gleaming like points of light in the darkness.

Eyes. In the dark.

Miriam's pulse began to beat faster, as though her body had shifted up a gear. *That's got nothing to do with it*, she thought quickly. *It's only an image of a rat. They're not real eyes.* But her pulse was still pounding and, beside her, she heard Stuart swallow noisily.

'Brilliant, isn't it?' he muttered.

Then the rat moved. Suddenly—between one pulse beat and the next—it darted forward, scuttling along the wall and round the corner towards them.

'Watch out!' Stuart shrieked.

He spun round again, following the rat's jerky progress, and Miriam spun too, without thinking, trying to keep the rat in sight as it ran and stopped and ran again.

But the pictures in front of her eyes couldn't keep pace. They jerked differently, completely out of time with her movements, and she felt her stomach lurch again. And again.

No. Not that.

13

She hadn't been car-sick for years, but she recognized the feeling. And she knew that she had to be still at once, before it was too late. Staggering slightly, she dragged her body back in the other direction, to kill the momentum and stop herself dead.

That was the worst mistake of all, because the pictures went on moving. For a split second, she was turning anti-clockwise while the images in front of her eyes still spun clockwise. Then she stopped and, dizzyingly, the room jerked backwards, making the movement she had just finished.

It was too much. She gagged at the back of her throat and, somewhere on her left, she saw Stuart turn and stare.

'Are you all right?'

She gagged again, jamming her hands hard up against her mouth, and heard Stuart laugh. A high, nervous laugh. The rat's feet scrabbled on the stones as it ran along the wall behind.

I can't, I can't . . . Her whole body was tense as she struggled to control it. *I can't* . . .

Then Hesketh's hand was on the back of her neck, wrenching at the clasp of the Game Helmet. And his other hand was over her right wrist, pulling the arm away from her mouth.

'*Don't* be sick on the glove,' he was muttering impatiently.

'I . . .'

It was over. Hesketh tugged the helmet off and suddenly the whole dungeon vanished. The grim walls, the bright green slime, the horrible, drooling rat. Gone. She was standing in the test room, taking long, deep breaths and avoiding Hesketh's eyes.

Turning away from her, Hesketh bent down to slip the helmet into the case. 'It does make some people motion-sick,' he said casually. 'Just close your eyes if you move quickly.'

14

Miriam frowned. 'I haven't been car-sick since I was a little girl. It makes me feel like a baby.'

'Takes you back, does it?'

There was something odd in Hesketh's voice. He was still kneeling on the floor, looking up with a faint, pleased smile. But what was there to be pleased about?

He didn't explain. Instead, he took hold of Miriam's hand and began to unfasten the glove. 'Don't worry about it. You'll be fine next time.'

'*Next* time?' Miriam imagined going back into the dungeon. Imagined Stuart's grey shape looking at her, with no face to show what it was thinking. 'I'm not sure if I want to try again.'

Hesketh raised an eyebrow. 'Not used to feeling stupid?'

'I'm . . .' It sounded arrogant to say, *No, I'm not.* But it was true.

Hesketh's mouth twitched. 'You'll be surprised at what you can do in the New World. Behind a mask.'

That was like being preached at. Miriam scowled. 'I think you'd be better off with someone else in your test.'

For a second Hesketh's fingers hesitated on the glove, then he smiled lightly. 'Oh no, I wouldn't. No one else will do.'

'Why not? There are dozens of fourteen year olds who *don't* get car-sick.'

Hesketh pulled the glove off with a single, sharp tug. 'I don't want any other fourteen year old. It has to be you. Now take those bracelets off, and you can go home.'

Miriam clicked them open and unbuckled the belt, watching them slide into their places. Hesketh didn't say another word until everything was packed away. Then he glanced round.

'See you on Friday?'

'I—'

'Or are you so grand you can't laugh at yourself?'

Miriam stiffened. 'Of course not. I'll be fine.'

'Good girl,' Hesketh said. He stretched out his right hand and, very lightly, laid his forefinger on her mouth. 'Not a word to anyone then. Remember? Not even your parents.'

And he snapped the lid of the case shut and flicked the catches down.

It was only later that Miriam realized what an odd conversation that was, after Hesketh had ushered her through the Research and Development department, and said goodbye at the front of the building. As she sat on the bus, rattling round the Ring Road and down into town, towards the river, the words started to buzz inside her head. *No one else will do . . . It has to be you.*

What was so special about her?

Pressing her face to the glass, she rolled the words round and round in her memory, but they didn't make any sense. Hesketh had met her that afternoon, for the first time. How could she be so important to the tests?

She was still puzzling when she got off the bus and walked down the towpath, towards the boat. But when she stepped aboard, the noise of her family hit her, driving everything else out of her head. A loud, quarrelsome noise, accompanied by a smell of raw fish.

Laura, her stepmother, was playing Monopoly in the main cabin, with Joe. They were squabbling at the tops of their voices.

'It's *mine*! I always have Mayfair!'

'Don't be such a *baby*, Joe. I'm not going to play if you cheat.'

'I've got all the rest of the set, and Miriam always lets me — '

'I don't *believe* it! Here's Miriam now. I'm going to ask her. Mim, darling — '

But before the question was out, Rachel came strutting through the door of the back cabin, draped in Miriam's black skirt and Miriam's best, precious red blouse.

16

'Look, don't they suit me? And I *need* something like this for Friday. Please, dear, darling Mim, can I — ?'

Laura shrieked. 'You're *not* to cadge Miriam's clothes! She hasn't got half as many as she ought to have anyway, and if you keep pinching them — '

Miriam ignored them and stuck her head into the galley. 'Hi, Dad.'

Her father was rolling herrings in oatmeal, his favourite economy for the end of the month. He looked up at her with his gentle, unobtrusive smile. 'Hallo, Minnow. How did it go?'

'Fine, thanks. Want any help?'

Her father smiled again and shook his head as Joe bellowed louder. 'I think they need you more than I do.'

Miriam pulled a face. Looking round into the main cabin, she raised her voice above the noise.

'No, you can't have Mayfair, Joe,' she said briskly. '*I* don't mind, but you know Laura cares about winning. And you *can* borrow my skirt, Rachel. I don't mind. But you don't need the blouse, because you've got that green one you haven't worn at all.'

That should fix them. Without leaving time for any more moans, she slipped backwards, past her father and into the back cabin that she shared with Rachel. She had just begun to scoop up the clothes — her clothes — that were scattered all over the floor when the door opened and Laura slid in.

'Well done, Mim. Joe's sulking now, so I don't have to go on with that *boring* game. I can hide in here, and hear all about your lovely afternoon.'

Miriam dumped the clothes into the cupboard. 'It was fine.'

'Darling, that's not telling! What happened? And how did you feel?'

That was what Laura always wanted to know. As though you hadn't done something unless you chewed it over and over endlessly afterwards. Sometimes Miriam couldn't bear it. Especially on days like today, when she had no intention of telling all the gory details.

'You know I'm not allowed to talk about the tests.'

'Oh, come on. No one's going to care if you tell me.'

For a moment, Miriam wavered. Then she remembered the feel of Hesketh's finger on her mouth, swearing her to silence.

'I'm not allowed to talk to *anyone*,' she said firmly.

Laura's eyebrows shot up and Miriam thought she might be going to insist. But she didn't. She stood up and shrugged.

'OK. Please yourself.'

Then she had gone. For a second, Miriam listened with her head on one side, to make sure that no one else was coming. It sounded safe enough. Joe was quarrelling with Rachel now, and Laura was in the galley, talking about some film or other, in a loud voice to show she didn't care. Rummaging under her bunk, Miriam pulled out a letter and sat down to read it.

Dear Miriam Enderby,

I am writing on behalf of the Research and Development Director at K & K Electronic Games to offer you an exciting opportunity.

As I am sure you know, we are the fastest-growing games company in the country, and our games are always tested extensively and thoroughly before they are put on the market. We are currently looking for a fourteen-year-old girl to take part in the testing of an important new project. Your name has been selected at random from a list, and we hope you will help us . . .

What do you expect? Laura had said. *If you fill in forms in those stupid magazines of yours, you're bound to get all sorts of junk.* Then she'd leant over and read the letter. *This one looks quite interesting, though. Why don't you give this Christine Riley woman a ring?*

That was how it had all started. The letter from Christine Riley, and then the phone call. After that, there hadn't been any reason to look at the letter again, and she'd almost forgotten exactly what it said.

Until now.

Miriam ran her finger over the words. *Your name has been selected at random* . . . But what had Hesketh said? Something about how important she was. About how no one else would do. That didn't fit in at all, unless she'd misunderstood him.

For a moment, she frowned, trying to recapture his exact words. But before she could remember them, Rachel erupted into the bedroom, wrenching at the red blouse and yelling over her shoulder.

' — and anyway it's not fair, because Mim has hundreds more clothes than me and she never goes out — '

Sliding the letter quickly back into its envelope, Miriam slipped it down the side of her bunk. Then she jumped up to rescue her blouse, before Rachel ruined it for ever.

Chapter 3

The noise that woke Will came much later, in the middle of the night. He opened his eyes and saw his father standing in the doorway, quite silent, a solid black shape against the almost-black of the hall.

'What's up?'

The shape shrugged and turned away, and Will sat up, propping himself on one elbow.

'I left you some dinner. Did you see the note?'

'Fine,' his father said, as though he hadn't really heard. 'Don't fuss. Go back to sleep, or you'll be late for school tomorrow.'

Wow. Will didn't say it out loud, but it would have been fair comment. He'd put up with nine weeks of silence, with just the odd grunt and a few messages left on the scratch pad. And then — *you'll be late for school tomorrow.* Really great conversation. Sometimes he wished he didn't have a genius for a father.

Slipping out of bed, he padded across to the door. 'Come on. What's up?'

His father slumped against the door frame. Even in the dark, Will sensed how tired he was. 'There's something going on. Something big. And I can't figure it out.'

'A game?' Will said quickly.

'A kind of game.'

'So what's the mystery? Whose game is it?'

There was a faint sound. A laugh, maybe, or a snort. 'Who cares? I haven't spent the last six weeks trying to find a name and address. I want to know what the game's all about. Why I can only access it when it's running on line, in real time.'

Will peered through the shadows, trying to see his face. 'You've been hacking into it?'

20

'When I can. But it's not backed up on to any hard disk that I can find. I can get into the system whenever I like, but when the game's not running — it vanishes. And when it *is* running, I can't make head or tail of it.'

'Want me to sort it out for you?' Will said lightly.

He meant it as a joke, but he felt his father stop breathing for a moment. And all at once, it wasn't a joke at all. Because even though his father was brilliant — the best — they both knew that Will was even better at actually playing the games.

In quite a different voice, he said, 'Do you want me to try?'

The black shape moved against the door post, standing suddenly upright. But there was no sound. He just stood there motionless. Will walked across to the window and leaned his face against the glass. He could see the rooftops of the houses in the road behind, outlined against the sky. For a moment, he thought about honesty. And danger.

Then he said, 'Is it important?'

'The most important thing since I've been in the business,' said the dark voice from the doorway. 'If I don't get a grip on it, I could be out of a job.'

Slowly, Will ran a finger down the glass. 'When would I have to play? If I decided to do it?'

'Monday, Wednesday, and Friday. Four-thirty to five.'

Like a dancing class. *Pink tights tomorrow at half-past four.* Will stood up straight and glanced over his shoulder. 'I'll try if you like. I've never hit a game yet that I can't crack.'

'You've got a better chance than anyone else. But it's dangerous stuff.'

'Think I can't keep my mouth shut?'

'Just be careful,' the black shape said.

And then, without any warning, it reached out and flicked on the light, so that Will was caught in the glare, tousled and blinking.

'Shall I set it up for you, then?' his father said, softly.

Throwing his head up, Will looked him straight in the eye, pretending that he wasn't dazzled. 'I'll start on Friday.'

21

K & K: ELECTRONIC MEMO
JOHN SHELLEY TO HESKETH BARRINGTON
PRIORITY: URGENT

Two MONTHS? Dream on, Hesketh. I might just be able to get you one month — if I twist a lot of arms — but I've got Accounts and Marketing breathing down my neck. We need to start selling New World NOW, not some time next year. We've got a lead over all our competitors, and we're not going to throw that away.

That means your security has to be perfect. Are you sure your Subjects are reliable?

Keep me up to date. I know you like to play things close to your chest, but this is too big to fool around with. Every time I think about the money hanging on it, I get the cold shakes.

K & K: ELECTRONIC MEMO
HESKETH BARRINGTON TO JOHN SHELLEY
PRIORITY: NORMAL

OK, I'll try and get through in a month.

Security is ALWAYS perfect in my department. Don't panic. Nothing's going to go wrong.

Chapter 4

Twenty-four hours later, Miriam woke up suddenly, in the early, dark hours of Friday morning. The shock of the nightmare jolted her out of sleep, and she woke to find herself lying cold and rigid, with the pillow clutched to her chest.

For a minute or more, she lay paralysed, listening to Rachel's soft snoring and the *glock glock glock* of the water against the side of the boat. Her heart raced, and the back of her neck was cold with sour sweat, but she didn't make a sound.

She never made a sound.

As the dread seeped out of her, she sat up slowly and leaned back, limp and exhausted, against the wall of the cabin. It was always the same nightmare. Not often, maybe not more than once or twice a year, but always the same, for as long as she could remember.

And the terror never grew less. Only now she knew, as soon as she woke, that it was no use struggling against the aftershock. She had to keep still until it ebbed away. Then she could sit up, and wait for the dream to fade.

It was fifteen or twenty minutes before she was ready to lie down again, and then she deliberately avoided thinking about the dream. Instead, she conjured up a picture of the bleak New World dungeon. The green slime. The locked door. The huddled skeleton and the rusty instruments of torture.

Inch by inch, she worked round it in her mind, forcing herself to remember every detail. Somewhere in that dungeon, behind a stone or hidden in a corner, there was a key, waiting to be found. If she was going back, she wanted to be the one who found it. *Think. Think.*

When she fell asleep again, she was smiling.

23

* * *

Getting away from Debbie was even worse on Friday.

'Not *again*! I thought you said it was a short course?'

'It *is* short,' Miriam said patiently. 'That's why I mustn't miss any of it.'

'But I thought you were coming round to my house.'

'I can't, Debs.'

'You must. I told Karen we'd fix her puppet theatre for her today. I *promised*.'

Miriam gave a small, bleak grin. Debbie's little sister was good fun, and she and Debbie had made some really cunning plans for the puppet theatre. But she had a promise of her own to keep.

And anyway, there was the key.

'I'd come if I could,' she said. Half-truthfully. 'Can't we do it tomorrow?'

'Not unless you want Karen to scream herself to sleep tonight.'

'Well, maybe we could—'

'Don't *bother*. I'm sure I can find someone else to help.'

Pointedly, Debbie stopped at the gate, to wait for Stella, and Miriam dragged her feet a bit as she marched off to the bus stop.

But with every step she took, it was more of a charade. Because she was actually looking forward to going, in spite of what had happened last time. Even if they hadn't been paying her, she would still have been waiting for the bus. Longing for it to be there. Because the game was so . . . so . . .

There wasn't a word in Miriam's head to describe it, but as Connie swooped past on her bike, free and fast, she thought, *Yes — that! That's what it's like!* And she fretted at the bus stop, impatient to be on her way. No, to be *there* — pulling on her helmet and standing in the horrible, gruesome dungeon. Why didn't the bus *come?*

24

It was ten minutes late. When she ran up the steps of the K & K building and into reception, Hesketh raised an eyebrow.

'Cold feet?'

'Of course not,' Miriam said quickly.

'You're happy to go and play?'

'I can't *wait*!'

She said it extravagantly, imitating Laura, but it wasn't really a joke. And Hesketh didn't treat it like one. With an approving nod, he hustled her off through the glittering centre of the building and into R & D, his secret kingdom of windowless, carpeted corridors.

'You're on your own today,' he said, as he swiped his plastic pass down the slot. 'In you go.'

'By myself?' Miriam looked at the Game Tower on the far side of the room. 'But suppose I break something?'

'You think you can?' Hesketh said scornfully. 'This game was built to stand up to nine-year old tearaways. How could you treat it worse than they will?'

'It doesn't matter if I trip over the tower, or tug the wires?'

'You could push a jam sandwich into the game slot,' Hesketh said impatiently. 'Or pour orange squash into all the cracks. This thing's as indestructible as Mount Everest. Now get a move on. Log in.'

He didn't leave immediately. He stood in the doorway watching as she rattled her name on to the keyboard and opened the black case. But he didn't say a word until she started fixing the Game Glove.

Then he murmured, 'Don't forget. Next to your skin.'

His voice was light and he spoke without looking at her, but Miriam frowned. As she wriggled her fingers into the glove, she studied it carefully, but there was nothing to see. And before she could look up again, the door closed and Hesketh had gone.

Flexing her fingers, she picked up the helmet with its two blank screens. As she ducked her head to slip it on, her heart give a quick little skip. *Now!*

Then she pushed the two sides of the clasp together, and she was back in the dungeon.

There was no sign of Stuart, but she didn't care about him. She had everything planned out in her head, and she was going to get on with it, without waiting. Lifting her right hand, she pointed at the heaped instruments of torture in the far corner.

As she glided towards them, she leant forward and peered, trying to make out the different shapes. There were ugly, distorted blades. Heavy chains and cruel, spiked fetters. Even a sort of man-trap, with two gaping jaws set with huge teeth. If they'd been real, Miriam would have shuddered and shrunk away from them.

But they weren't real. They didn't matter at all. The only thing that mattered was that other shape which might be tangled in with them. The long, straight shaft, with a looped top and a jagged, zigzag end.

And there it was!

She saw it from a couple of metres away. A big, rusty key, at the back of the pile. Right behind the man-trap.

The moment she was close enough, she shot out her right hand, aiming straight through the jaws of the man-trap to grab at the key. But, as her fingers darted between the gigantic, threatening teeth, everything changed.

It happened in a flash. She was almost there, with her fingers virtually touching the key, when the man-trap came horribly, terrifyingly alive. Suddenly, the key and the man-trap vanished, and Miriam saw her hand disappearing between the jaws of the giant rat.

Like lightning, she snatched it back, just as the fanged jaws crashed shut. Instantly, the rat disappeared, and she found herself staring at the man-trap and the key.

It was an illusion. That was all. She moved her hand forward again.

Grrr!

Instantly, the rat was there again, snarling and red-eyed. This time, she only just made it. As she pulled her hand back, she felt the rat's mouth brush the ends of her fingers.

She was nursing her hand, and staring at the key, when a grey shape appeared beside her.

'You worked it out too!' said Stuart's voice. He sounded out of breath and disappointed. 'I thought I was going to beat you to it, but Christine was stuck in the traffic. She's only just got here.'

'It's not that simple,' Miriam muttered. 'Look.'

She moved her hand again, to show Stuart, and he jumped back as the rat's teeth clashed together.

'That's pretty good,' he said, admiringly. 'How are we going to get out of that? Maybe we need something to distract it.' His head turned as he stared round the dungeon, and suddenly he gave a delighted yelp. 'How about a bone?'

'A — ?' For a second, Miriam couldn't work out what he meant.

'The skeleton!' he said, impatiently. 'Let's give the rat one of its bones.'

'But that's *disgusting*!' Miriam pulled a face. 'We can't be meant to do that.'

Stuart snorted. 'No? You haven't played many games, have you?'

He marched across the dungeon and picked up one of the big thigh bones. There was something defiant about the way he walked back towards Miriam. He was only a blank grey shape, but she could see that he was offended. He held the bone out at arm's length.

'Wave this in front of its face to keep it busy. I'll try and sneak my hand into its mouth.'

27

No, you won't, thought Miriam. She had worked out where the key was, and she meant to get it herself. '*You* wave the bone,' she said.

Stuart snorted again, as though he might be going to argue, but he didn't. Crouching down, he held the bone a few inches away from the man-trap.

'Go on, then,' he said. 'But be careful. This may not work.'

Miriam knelt down and concentrated for a second. Then, very slowly and smoothly, she moved her hand towards the man-trap.

Grrr!

It took all her will-power to keep the hand steady as the rat's face appeared. The points of its teeth were very sharp, and very close to her fingers.

But Stuart was right. As he waved the bone, very gently, the rat's eyes slid sideways, watching it.

'Now!' he whispered. 'But keep it very slow.'

Holding her breath, Miriam moved her hand forward, millimetre by millimetre, watching the rat's eyes all the time. They didn't move from the bone. If she was careful, she could do it. Slowly . . .

And then the whispering began.

. . . *min-na, min-na, min-na* . . .

It was very soft, almost indistinguishable. But there was something odd about it. For a second she was distracted, trying to make out the words, and her hand wobbled.

'Careful!' hissed Stuart.

The rat's eyes slid sideways, and for one dreadful second Miriam thought he was going to bite her hand off.

. . . *min-na, min-na* . . .

Her heart thudded and she could feel the pulse pounding in her neck, but somehow she steadied the hand and kept it where it was. Stuart waved the bone again and, slowly, the rat's eyes swivelled back towards it.

An instant later, Miriam felt something in the darkness behind the rat's teeth. She couldn't see it, but her fingers closed round a long, narrow shaft and she took a deep breath.

Now!

Jerking backwards—so hard that she sprawled on the carpet of the test room—she snatched the key out of the rat's mouth, clutching it triumphantly to her chest.

Immediately, the whispering stopped and the rat disappeared. Miriam found herself staring at the rusty man-trap, and the big studded door beyond.

Stuart held out his hand for the key. 'Well done. Toss it over and I'll unlock the door.'

You've got to be joking, Miriam thought. She wasn't having any of that. It was her key, and she was going to open the door. Gliding across, she pushed it into the lock and turned her hand.

Immediately, there was a fanfare of trumpets. The door swung open, and enormous yellow letters blazed in front of her eyes.

WELL DONE, MIRIAM!
500 POINTS

Behind the blank grey mask of her face, she grinned like an idiot. Then she stepped through the open door, ahead of Stuart.

Chapter 5

The room beyond was quite different from the dungeon. It was delicate and elegant, with eight sides and a high, domed roof. Across its angled walls moved a glittering rainbow of constantly changing colours.

In the centre of each of the eight walls was a wide, arched door. The one that Miriam and Stuart had just unlocked was blue on the inside and the others were all different, bright colours, ranging from dark indigo to a spotless, brilliant white.

Looking up, Miriam saw a crystal chandelier hanging from the ceiling, dozens of feet above her head. The rest of the room was empty, except for a square glass case, set on a wooden column in the centre of the floor. There was a jagged hole in one of the side windows of the case.

'Come on,' she said. 'Let's take a look at that.'

Raising her arm, she pointed at the glass case, trying to reach it before Stuart. He might know more about computer games than she did, but she had scored first. And it would be good to stay ahead.

They were half-way there when there was a huge flash. Thunder cracked from the eight corners of the room and a deep voice boomed at them.

Do not come nearer, unless you are ready to seek the Rainbow Crystal!

'That sounds promising!' Stuart said, enthusiastically. 'Watch out though, in case it's a trap.'

Miriam was already watching as hard as she could. Ever since the rat's teeth had clashed against her fingers, she had been tense and alert, poised on a knife-edge of concentration. As she moved forward towards the case, she was aware of every inch of the rainbow room. Every flicker of light, and every whisper.

30

She stopped beside the jagged, smashed pane and Stuart slid up next to her. Together they peered through the hole, gazing at the shiny blue cushion inside. There was a dent in the centre of it, as though something had been taken away.

Then the deep voice boomed again.

Until the Crystal is found, reality will be changeable and unreliable.

'So what do we do?' Miriam called out. 'How can we find it?'

Stuart snorted. 'It's not a person. It's a computer-generated voice. There's no point in talking back to it, because there's no one there to understand.'

Was that a sneer? Miriam looked round sharply, but the grey oval of his face was as blank as ever. Ignoring him, she began to move round the glass case.

On the far side, on the wooden stand, was a small black lever. Miriam reached out her right hand and curled the fingers round it.

'Careful!' Stuart said nervously.

'I *am* being careful.' Miriam pulled the lever firmly towards her and, for the third time, the great voice boomed out.

If you are ready, you must start by finding the map.

As though that had been a signal, the room began to move. Slowly at first, and then faster and faster, it started to spin around them, as though it were a great wheel, turning on the wooden column at the centre. The doors slid past, one after another, moving clockwise until the colours merged together and disappeared in a blur of dazzling light.

Miriam squeezed her eyes shut, knowing she would be sick if she tried to watch that spinning, but she didn't relax for an instant. Her body was still geared up for action, exhilarated and triumphant. Her pulse raced, and she could feel every heartbeat and every breath, as she waited for whatever would happen next.

Then she heard Stuart say, 'Oh!' and she opened her eyes.

Away to her left, one of the doors—the orange one—had swung wide. Through it, she could see a bright sun glaring down on to a totally unexpected landscape.

Tall, forked cacti, with exaggerated spikes, were dotted over a narrow strip of dusty brown earth. On either side, cliffs reared up vertically. They towered into canyon walls and, from way up at the top of the canyon, smoke rose in lazy, intermittent puffs.

Something rolled jerkily in front of the doorway. A ball of awkward strands, like a curled-up spider. For a second Stuart stiffened nervously and then he gave a light, silly laugh.

'It's—what's it called?—tumbleweed, isn't it?' He sounded almost relieved.

Miriam stared at the tumbleweed blowing up the canyon. It had nothing to do with the dungeon they had just left. This was a completely different world.

Cartoon cowboy land. The Wild West.

'Howdy,' drawled a hoarse voice from the threshold.

And there was the cowboy himself. Drooping moustache. Ten gallon hat. Spurs a foot long and leather chaps flapping round his legs. He leaned against the doorpost, grinning at them and twirling a six-shooter on one outstretched finger.

Miriam went on staring. To her, he seemed like another piece of the landscape. The final cartoon touch. But Stuart reacted quite differently. He launched himself forward, with a yelp.

'Weapons! That's what we need!'

Before Miriam could take in what he meant, he was standing in the doorway, reaching out for the gun. The cowboy spat sideways into the dust, twirled faster—and then flung the gun high into the air.

32

Stuart leaned forward and snatched, grabbing at the gun as it fell. The moment he touched it, his blank grey body fizzed, as though it had been electrified.

A trap! Miriam thought.

But she was wrong. When the fizzing cleared, she found herself facing two cowboys. Next to the original pot-bellied man with the moustache stood a tall, lean figure, dressed in black. He had a white, ruffled shirt, a fancy waistcoat and a black bootlace tie. Along his top lip spread a narrow, dark moustache.

'Stuart?' Miriam said.

The new cowboy craned his head comically, trying to get a proper look at his own body. 'Hey! That's great!'

The original cowboy pulled another gun from his left holster. Without a word, he began to spin it on one finger, just as he had spun the first gun.

'That's yours,' Stuart said. 'Don't worry about catching it perfectly. All I did was touch mine with one finger.'

He was trying to be helpful. Trying to organize her and take her over, the way Laura did. Miriam gritted her teeth.

'I'm fine, thank you.'

And she would have been fine — she *would* — if he hadn't distracted her. If he'd just left her alone, she would have caught the gun as easily as he had. But she was so determined not to be beaten that she forgot all about the time lag.

The moment the cowboy threw the gun into the air, she launched herself straight for it, as though it were a real weapon, falling to the real ground in front of her. She darted her hand at the place where she could see it, expecting to feel its hard shape under her fingers.

But her grey ghostly hand, in the game, didn't react as fast as her real hand. By the time it moved, a split second later, the gun had already fallen below the place where she aimed. Her fingers closed round empty air, and she heard the gun clatter to the ground at her feet.

33

'Quick!' Stuart said urgently. 'Pick it up before he can get it back!'

'All *right*!' Miriam felt she would say something rude if he kept treating her like a baby. 'Of course I'm going to pick it up.'

She bent down, with her hand outstretched, ready to snatch up the gun . . .

Chapter 6

. . . and Will, in front of his computer screen, leaned forward and clutched the mouse tighter.

Until that moment, the game had been utterly boring and frustrating. All he could see were two dull grey sprites gliding from one background to another. They kept squeaking in shrill, garbled voices, like strangled mice, and he couldn't make any sense out of the noise — or even decide if it was supposed to make sense. And he hadn't got a clue what he was supposed to do.

The backgrounds were OK — especially the dungeon — but nothing he tried had any effect on the picture. The keyboard was useless and even the mouse just gave him a scarlet arrow that danced all over the screen. He pressed all three of its buttons, but they didn't seem to *do* anything. He wasn't surprised the thing had baffled his father. Maybe it wasn't a game at all. He scowled at the screen.

And especially at the little grey sprites. He hated the way they glided around, not taking any notice of anything he did, and their squeaking was starting to drive him mad.

Then the orange door swung open, and the cowboy appeared.

Suddenly, for no obvious reason, Will felt more cheerful. He sat up straighter and watched the cowboy lounging in the doorway. Now that was a character *worth* having as an enemy. Maybe it would be a good idea to try the arrow again.

The figure began to twirl a gun on one finger, and Will attacked with his mouse. He aimed the arrow at the cowboy's belly and clicked furiously, trying all the buttons — left, centre, right.

Still no effect.

OK. That was *it.* He was going to give the whole thing up. Phone his father at work and tell him he couldn't do it. And never mind how stupid that made him look.

Then the gun went flying up into the air and one of the grey sprites reached out and grabbed it.

ZAP!

With a crackle and a fizz of stars, the faceless grey sprite changed completely. Will found himself staring at a cartoon cardsharper, with a tie like a bootlace and a moustache like the tie.

Suddenly, with that eerie sixth sense that came to him when he was playing, he knew he had seen something crucial. As the sprite stepped past the cowboy, into the next background, his brain was whirring.

That gun was the key. The passport that took the sprites through the door. He was ready to bet that there would be a second gun, for the other grey sprite.

But suppose it didn't catch the gun?

Will found himself grinning idiotically. Those guns were vital. If he was ever going to get into the game, he had to do it that way. Maybe the mouse would finally have some effect, if he clicked on the gun.

As the scruffy cowboy pulled its second sixshooter from the holster, Will leaned forward, his fingers poised over the mouse, concentrating so hard that he barely blinked. He *had* to get that gun. It twirled round and round on the cowboy's finger. Round and round and —

Now!

The moment the gun flew up into the air, he pounced, sliding the scarlet arrow on to the falling shape and clicking.

Nothing happened.

But the grey sprite seemed to have missed too. Great. That meant the game was giving him a second chance. Quick as a flash, Will slid the arrow down the screen, so that it rested right on the gun, with its tip touching a bundle of tumbleweed. *Click! Click! Click!*

This time, something did happen, but it wasn't what he had expected. All he was trying to do was pick up the gun, but his mouse still didn't have any effect on that.

Instead, as he clicked the third button, on the right, he discovered what he should have been aiming for. The tumbleweed. The clump under the tip of the arrow changed suddenly, twisting into quite a different shape.

The grey, tangled stems writhed and straightened, forming themselves into a groping, disembodied hand. And almost before the hand was complete, its fingers snapped together, closing round the gun while the grey sprite was still bending towards it. Then, like lightning, they jerked it backwards — and vanished.

'Yes!'

A little box flashed up at the top right of the screen, and Will shouted out loud as he saw a score in it. 10 POINTS. He'd done it! He'd found a gateway into the game!

And what he'd done was obviously right. There was no other gun for the second grey sprite. Instead, while the score was still flashing, the screen erupted. There was a thunder of hoofs and a rat-tat-tat of spattering bullets, and three masked figures came galloping down the canyon.

Their guns blazed, spouting comic little tufts of flame as they fired, and the bullets ricocheted from one red rock to another with a cheerful *twang*.

The sprites in the doorway leapt into life, whirling round to face the galloping bandits. The cardsharper fired back, leaning close against the doorframe, but the other sprite — the one that was still grey — had no weapon at all. As the gunmen advanced, it turned back to the door, trying to slip through into the octagonal room.

'Oh no, you don't!'

Will grinned again, and his mouse danced across the mat, shifting the red arrow on to the door. This time he was sure it would work. And it did. At the first click, the door swung shut.

No way out there for the grey sprite. No way out anywhere. There was another, huge burst of shots and, as it cowered back against the closed door, all the bandits fired at once.

Will saw the bullets hit the sprite, right in the centre of its body. A great gush of red fountained out of its chest, covering half the screen for a moment. When it cleared, Will saw the sprite slide down into a pool of blood and lie still.

50 POINTS flashed the score box.

He took a long breath. He was on his way. He didn't know what it was all about yet, or how many levels there were, but he knew that he had to defeat the squeaking little sprites.

And to do that, he had to discover where the weapons were. His weapons wouldn't be obvious ones, like the gun. They would be disguised as ordinary things, like clumps of tumbleweed. But once he'd worked out where they were, a simple click would strip away their disguises. All he had to do was think, and he was good at that.

His father wouldn't be disappointed after all.

Leaning closer, he stared at the screen, watching as the other sprite — the cardsharper — swaggered off down the canyon.

Chapter 7

'No!' Miriam yelled.

As the blood exploded out of her chest, she grabbed the clasp at the back of her Game Helmet. Ripping it open, she tore the helmet off and raced across to the Game Tower. She *wasn't* going to be pushed out of the game like that. She would just go back in and start again, at the beginning. Furiously, she tapped in her name on the keyboard, as fast as she could. M-I-R-I-A-M.

For a second, she thought it had worked. As she pulled the helmet on again and pushed the clasp shut, she saw the screens in front of her eyes flicker into life.

But it wasn't the castle dungeon that she saw. And it wasn't the rainbow room, or the Wild West. Just a steady green brightness, with solid, square letters ranged across it, like pillars of stone, a foot high.

SORRY, MIRIAM, YOU'RE DEAD.

SCORE SO FAR — 525 POINTS.

She smashed her hand at the letters, trying to knock them over. But nothing happened. She couldn't even see the grey shape of her hand in front of her. She was invisible, and the letters were untouched.

In the New World, she was dead.

For a second time, she pulled the helmet off and, as she dropped it on to the Game Tower, the door opened. A large, crumpled figure filled the doorway.

'What happened to you?' asked Hesketh.

Miriam scowled at him, and began to pull off the glove. 'I got shot. I'm dead.'

Hesketh shook his head. 'No need for that. You only had to catch the gun.'

'Well, I didn't catch it. I missed, and I got shot.'

'You should have picked it off the ground.' He came across the room to take the glove from her. In spite of his

39

bulk, he was bizarrely light on his feet. 'You had ten seconds to do that before the outlaws came.'

'No, I didn't!' Miriam said. 'That hand snatched it away.'

Hesketh had leaned over to pick up the case, and he had his back to her. 'Hand?' he said lightly.

'Yes.' Miriam stared at him. Surely he must know what she was talking about. 'The tumbleweed that changed into a hand. The way that man-trap changed into a rat.'

'I know about the rat. But . . . the tumbleweed?' Hesketh rocked back on to his heels and looked up at her. 'It's easy to imagine things when you get hassled.'

'I *didn't* imagine it. There was a hand. And it snatched the gun before I had a chance to get it.'

He didn't answer her. He just let her voice hang in the air, until she heard her own words and how they sounded. *It's not fair. I didn't have a chance. It wasn't my fault.* Moaning. Was that all it was? Could she, possibly, have been mistaken?

'There *was* a hand,' she said stubbornly. 'It was real.'

'Real?' Hesketh raised the other eyebrow and smiled. 'Which kind of reality? This one we're standing in now? Or the reality of the game?'

'I . . .' For a second, she thought he must be teasing her. 'That's stupid. There can't be different kinds of real.'

'No?' He tugged at his ear-ring, looking amused. 'So what happened when you tried to get back into the game just now? After you were dead? You were real in this room all right. Your feet were on the carpet, and you were breathing the air. But—in the game world?'

Miriam remembered lashing out at the stone letters. SORRY, MIRIAM, YOU'RE DEAD. By rights, she should have bruised her hand against them. That was what her brain had told her to expect. But . . . nothing.

Hesketh persisted. 'You weren't real there, were you? Not any more?'

She looked away from him. 'That doesn't mean anything. Real is real. Computer games are just pretending.'

'You mean they don't matter?' Hesketh smiled, annoyingly. 'You don't care what happens while you're playing?' He held out his hand for the bracelets, and Miriam pulled them off and dropped them unceremoniously into the case.

'No point in caring, is there?' she said. 'What do I do now? Just go home?'

'Until Monday.' Hesketh clicked the case shut.

'Don't I . . . stay dead?'

'Only if you want to.'

Why shouldn't she want to? It was the second time the game had made a fool of her. Why should she waste three afternoons a week being beaten by a boy like Stuart? If she had any sense — and she had plenty — she would just toss her head and tell Hesketh that she wasn't coming back.

Except that . . . she wanted to come back. She wanted to be back in the game *now*, this minute, without having to wait until the next session. She could strike all the poses she liked, but she knew she would be there on Monday. And Hesketh knew it too. He chuckled suddenly, his heavy face cracking into a clown's grin, so that Miriam had to grin back.

But that didn't do anything to lift her spirits. As she walked out of the building, she felt disappointed. She'd played badly, and now it was over and she would have to wait three whole days for another chance.

Ahead of her, the road to the bus stop stretched dull in the twilight. Dusty bushes, with half their leaves fallen, straggled beside the dirty pavements, and the tarmac was pitted with potholes. Everything she could see was blurred by the dusk. Blurred and without interest, as though some giant had sucked the life out of it.

She stopped and looked back, over her shoulder. The huge slab of the K & K building was dull and dirty too, made of bricks as lifeless as the tarmac. But from inside, at every glittering window, it was lit by sharp fluorescent light.

It glowed like a chest of fairy treasure. A box crammed with magic secrets that it couldn't contain. At every crack and through every window, it leaked energy and brilliance, and Miriam was scorched by such longing that she could hardly breathe.

She wanted to stand there gazing, until the doors opened again. Until she could get back into the New World where she had been really alive and awake.

And then she remembered that she wasn't alive there at all just now. She was dead. Wryly, she turned away and walked down the road, forbidding herself to think about the game until she was safe in the warm fug of the bus.

Even then, she tried to keep her mind on ordinary, practical things. Pulling out her rough notebook, she started her homework, struggling to come up with headlines about the Battle of Hastings. (*Arrow Shoots Willy to Top. Harold Conqs Out.*) But long before they reached the river she was staring out of the window, running the last moments of the game over and over in her head.

The cowboy had thrown the gun up in the air.

She had grabbed and missed.

Immediately, while the gun was still thudding to the ground, she had stooped down to pick it out of the clump of tumbleweed.

And then the tumbleweed had changed into a hand.

She *wasn't* mistaken. Before she could reach it, the tumbleweed had twisted suddenly, forming itself into gnarled, long fingers that curled round the gun and snatched it into nowhere. That was how it had been. She wasn't going to let Hesketh convince her she'd imagined it.

And yet . . . it was his game. He'd invented it and been in charge of developing it, and he was running the tests. If he hadn't put the hand there — who had?

42

*　*　*

It was her father who saw she had something on her mind. But he didn't jump on her the way the others would have done, if they'd noticed. ('Hallo, grumps. What's up?' 'Mim! Why aren't you listening?' 'Are you feeling all right, darling?') He waited until after tea.

Immediately the meal was over, Laura leapt out of her seat. 'Oh, *bum*! I'm going to be late for aerobics again! And I'm so full up I'll probably be sick when I *do* get there.'

She raced off to the car and departed, with much revving of the ancient, noisy engine, and suddenly the boat was very quiet. Quiet and rather chilly. Rachel and Joe settled down to squabble over the television and Miriam retreated to the back cabin, spreading out her homework on the bunk and trying not to think about guns and tumbleweed.

She was failing miserably when her father stuck his head round the door.

'Washing-up?' he said, with his faint, mild smile.

It was Rachel's turn, not hers, and it wasn't like her father to ask anyway, but Miriam didn't quibble. Anything was better than sitting there with her thoughts going round in a treadmill. And washing-up couldn't be duller than the Battle of Hastings. Pushing her books back into the bag, she slid out to the galley.

Even then, her father didn't ask her anything straight away. He moved round peacefully, scraping plates into the bin, stacking dirty dishes and drying clean ones, while Miriam scrubbed briskly at the sink.

They were on the last few saucepans before he said, 'This "computer course", Minnow — is it working out OK?'

She glanced sideways at him, surprised by the question. 'You know I can't tell you about it. I promised.'

'That doesn't mean . . .'

43

He paused, hunting for the right words. Wiping all the time at a saucepan, with steady, even strokes. Miriam watched the delicate, precise movements of his fingers.

'There's no point in telling me the technical details,' he said at last, with a deprecating smile. Like a lark apologizing for not knowing nuclear physics. 'And anyway, if you've made a promise, you must keep it. But if these tests are . . . upsetting . . . I don't think the promise ought to stop you telling me.'

He let the words trail away, looking gently down at her. Miriam thought, for the hundredth time, how unlike anyone else's father he was. How tentative and uncertain — and perceptive.

'I'm all right,' she said briskly. 'The game's very good, but it's difficult. That's all. I need to try and work things out while I'm not playing.'

He gave her a long, thoughtful stare and then squatted down to slide the saucepan on to its shelf.

'Don't underestimate it,' he murmured, with his back to her. 'Games are serious stuff, Minnow. And I don't want you to start having nightmares again.'

Miriam looked down at his bent head, wondering whether he really thought her nightmares had stopped. It was a very long time since she'd woken him up and he'd cradled her on his lap, letting her scream into his shoulder. Not since he'd married Laura, maybe.

But he didn't miss many things about her. *Do you know how often I still have that dream?* For a second, the question fluttered in her mind.

But she left it too long. Joe screamed suddenly from the main cabin and came rattling through with a roar.

'*Rachel* said — !'

The moment had gone. Miriam stepped back and her father stood up, glancing at her with a fleeting, regretful smile. Then Joe cannoned into them both, and Rachel came thundering after him, yelling at the top of her voice, to make herself heard above his screams.

K & K: ELECTRONIC MEMO
JOHN SHELLEY TO HESKETH BARRINGTON
PRIORITY: URGENT

For heaven's sake, what's going on? Report in please. I need to know how the tests are going.

Are you confident about security?

K & K: ELECTRONIC MEMO
HESKETH BARRINGTON TO JOHN SHELLEY
PRIORITY: NORMAL

Security in my department is always fine. Sir.

The tests are running like clockwork. (High speed clockwork.) Individual phobia patterns were checked out on Friday and Subject A (the girl) and Subject B (the boy) both reacted as predicted. They are already showing good signs of attachment to the game.

Chapter 8

It seemed a long weekend, and Miriam spent most of it in a dream.

She was haunted by her vision of the K & K building, that magic, light-filled box she had seen as she glanced back up the road. It was still there, waiting for her to go back. Holding the New World, ready for her to enter.

Until she could get there, all she wanted to do was sit and conjure up the scenes in her head — the dungeon, the rainbow room, the Wild West. She wanted to go over and over the things that had happened, enjoying them properly and trying to get the feel of the game into her blood.

But it was impossible to be private. Wherever she went, the boat was full of her family, and there were dozens of things she had to do. Supermarket shopping with Laura. Bedtime stories for Rachel and Joe. Washing up. *Talking.*

Especially talking. Laura never seemed to leave her alone. She was like a perpetual firework, always exploding with questions and jokes and comments, and every single one needed some kind of answer. On and on, until Miriam felt like screaming, *Leave me alone! Get out of my head! I want to think!*

It was a relief to go back to school on Monday.

Debbie had spent the weekend hanging around with Stella and a couple of boys from Asher's, and she was full of it. All she needed was a listener.

This one with red hair — Pete — he's a real devil. Doesn't care what he does. There's a boy at his school called Jojo, one of those brainy idiots, and Pete just teases him all the time. It's cruel really, but the way he tells it — well, you'd laugh too, Miriam. Honestly you would.

Miriam got by with a quarter of her usual attention, letting the words wash over her while most of her mind was somewhere else. Wandering through dungeons, and walking up red rock canyons with the tumbleweed blowing round her ankles.

But not everyone was as unobservant as Debbie. On Monday afternoon, Miriam came out of a daze, half-way through Double English, and saw Connie Baxter watching her curiously from the other side of the room. She wasn't at all embarrassed to be caught staring. She just arched her long neck and gave Miriam a lazy smile.

When the lesson was over, she came strolling across.

'You made me work hard today,' she drawled. 'I was the only one trying to liven things up. What happened to you? Got something on your mind?'

Miriam scrambled her books together, pushing them higgledy piggledy into her bag. Connie made her nervous. She went off on her own too much and liked things that nobody else liked. 'So what if I have? My mind's my own business.'

The moment she'd spoken, she knew it was a silly thing to say. Debbie would have jumped on it straight away, either as a joke (*Ooh, who is he?*) or with wide, sympathetic eyes. However she reacted, Miriam wouldn't have escaped without an explanation.

But Connie was different. If she had questions, she kept them to herself and bided her time. Even when she was Miriam's best friend, she had been detached and hard to understand, and she hadn't changed. Instead of trying to discover Miriam's thoughts, she nodded casually and swung her bag over her shoulder.

'I hope you're back on form next time. I can't keep Mrs Fussbags busy all on my own. I need you to argue with.' She was almost at the door when she turned and called over her shoulder. 'Oh, by the way, you were off in a dream when she was giving out the homework. Call me later on, and I'll tell you what she said.' She grinned. 'When you're back from that course you're so busy brooding about.'

47

Then she went, leaving Miriam blinking at the sheer — the sheer *Connieness* of what she'd done. She hadn't snooped. She'd hardly asked any questions. But she knew what was going on. She'd homed in on the crucial thing. And she'd even remembered that this was one of the 'computer course' days, when Miriam had no time to hang around and catch up on homework.

Which was more than Debbie had. When Miriam turned right at the school gates, she pulled a face and frowned.

'Monday as well? This course of yours is a real pain.'

'I told you — ' Miriam began, mildly.

But Debbie didn't give her a chance to finish. 'Well, I'm going to catch the others up. You know I hate walking home on my own.'

She scuttled off after Stella, waving and calling, and Miriam trudged the other way, watching for the bus. And for Christine Riley. Christine *mustn't* come before the bus today. Stuart had stolen a march on her last time, and it would be maddening if he sneaked in first today.

As the bus drew up, she jumped on before it had properly stopped, and when she got off at the Business Park she found herself running up the road to K & K.

Hesketh grinned when he saw her. 'You decided not to stay dead, did you?'

'I fancied a bit of resurrection,' Miriam said lightly. 'But where do I come to life again? Do I start again, back at the beginning?'

Hesketh stroked his ear-ring. 'You ought to, but we haven't got time for that. Not if we're going to meet our deadline. Christine's saved the game and you'll both start off together in the rainbow room.' He gave her a wide, bland smile. 'With the map.'

'Stuart found it?' Miriam pulled a face. 'I bet he raked in hundreds of points for that.'

Hesketh shrugged, 'He earned them. He's a pretty good player.'

48

Miriam tried to look impressed, but her feet gave her away. She strode through the building, half a pace ahead of Hesketh, impatient to get to the game. If she didn't score some real points in this session, she might just as well give up.

The instant he let her into the test room, she was heading for the Game Tower. Tugging on the kit, she logged in with one hand while she fixed her helmet with the other. Before Hesketh left, she was pushing the clip shut.

And she beat Stuart. Just. For a split second she was alone in the rainbow room, and she headed straight for the folded piece of paper that she saw on top of the glass case. She was going to get hold of that while she had the chance.

When she was half-way there, Stuart appeared on the far side of the room. His moustache and his fancy waistcoat had disappeared, and he was a simple grey shape again, like her.

'Hey!' he said.

Miriam didn't take any notice. Before he could move, she reached the glass case and grabbed at the piece of paper. It unfolded as she touched it and her heart gave a little skip. It was the map all right.

But not the sort of map she had expected. She'd imagined a storybook chart, with wind cherubs in the corners and dragons and sea monsters in uncharted places. This was a perfectly ordinary, rather crude map of the world, with the different continents in different colours. Blue Europe. Green Asia. Violet Africa. And not a single word written on it.

Stuart came up beside her, uncomfortably close. 'Peculiar, isn't it? I got a thousand points for winning it, but I haven't got a clue how to use it.'

'Well, we'd better work it out then.' Miriam hadn't meant to sound so snappy, but she wasn't going to have him showing off about how many points he had. She peered at the map. 'It has to be *some* use. The voice said we had to find it before we looked for the Crystal.'

'It didn't say we had to find *this* map. This one might be just a red herring. Game designers like things like that.'

Show-off, Miriam thought. But she didn't say a word. Stuart began to glide round the room, trying each of the coloured doors in turn, but none of them opened.

'Do you think we ought to try the black handle again?'

'Please yourself.' Miriam didn't care what he did. She was sure the map was the important thing, and she was determined to find out what it was for.

Stuart stretched out his grey, ghostly hand and Miriam saw it close round the handle. But before he could move it, the great voice boomed into the silence.

If you pull the handle again, the room will explode.

'Whoops!'

The hand jerked back, and Miriam grinned secretly. So much for showing off. This *was* the right map. She stared down at it, trying to find some hidden message, or a puzzle to crack. But it was just — the world. Green Asia, violet Africa, red Antarctica. Plain, bare patches of colour. What had those got to do with the room she was in? Or with the creepy castle, or the Wild West canyon?

Except . . . Idly, Miriam stretched out a finger and tapped the place where the Wild West would have been. The middle of the orange shape that was North America.

And something swam out of the orange towards her.

It swelled bigger and bigger, until it almost filled the screens in front of her eyes and her heart jumped triumphantly. *I knew it!*

Then she frowned again. Because all she was seeing was another copy of the map. Exactly the same as the one that was lying on the glass case.

Stuart could obviously see it too. 'What happened?' he muttered. 'What did you do?'

Miriam hesitated for a moment. But she didn't seem to be giving anything much away. 'I just touched North America. Because that was where we were last time.'

Stuart nodded. 'Where I found the map.'

Where—

They both realized together. At the same moment, their hands flashed out, smacking down side by side on to the blue shape in the middle of the map.

'Castles in Spain!' said Stuart. 'Europe!'

And a reddish-brown shape came floating up from the blue. Long and thin, with a ring at one end and a wide, jagged edge at the other. It was the key they had found in the castle.

The European castle.

Suddenly, the whole thing somersaulted into sense. Miriam forgot for a moment that she and Stuart were competing against each other.

'It's not a map to look at!' she yelled. 'It's a map to *use*—like a menu. Touching Europe shows us the key, because we found it there. And touching North America shows us the map. So—'

But already Stuart's arm was sliding sideways, towards a new continent. There was no time for Miriam to react or argue. Before she could say another word, his hand touched down, with the fingers spread wide, almost covering the red sprawl of Antarctica.

Another shape rose towards them, out of the map. Miriam's brain grappled with the image. Something brown and tangled, twisted in on itself.

A rope?

Before she could be sure, the room began to spin, exactly as it had last time, when she pulled the black handle. The doors rattled past. Green, blue, indigo, violet, whiteredorangeyellow—faster and faster—

Miriam had to shut her eyes, but she listened hard. Behind her eyelids, she held the image of Stuart's grey shape on the other side of the room, poised to leap

51

forward the instant the spinning stopped. She had to hear him move, or she would get left behind.

But he didn't leap forward.

Instead, he gasped. Miriam opened her eyes. The spinning had stopped all right, and the red door had swung back, almost out of sight. But Stuart hadn't moved. The glare that shone through the open door was so bright that Miriam had to put her hand up to shield her eyes.

'We can't go in there,' Stuart said, crossly. 'We'll damage our eyes. What's going on?'

'I — ' For a moment, Miriam was baffled too. It looked as though there was nothing through the door except pure, searing light.

And then she realized.

'That's what it looks like, with the sun on it. What did you expect to find in Antarctica, you idiot?'

'I — '

'It's *snow*!'

Chapter 9

Snow? Will's heart slumped. He stared at the screen in disgust as the two grey sprites stepped through the doorway into the white, featureless world.

What could he do with snow?

There was nothing else to be seen. No kind of weapon. Not a thing. Just a dead white screen. What was he meant to do? *Freeze* the sprites to death?

But even that was no good. As the two little figures stepped through the doorway, they were transformed instantly, changing from grey ghosts to Polar explorers. They were dressed from head to foot in bright, padded clothes, with snowshoes on their feet, and furry hoods and snow goggles hiding their faces.

Great! Will thought sarcastically. What chance did that leave him? Was he supposed to beat them to death with their own snowshoes?

He scanned the screen, inch by inch, but nothing broke the glaring white of the snow. Nothing except a line of footprints running from side to side of the screen, in the middle distance. And he couldn't pick up those and chuck them.

Then one of the sprites bent down and scooped up a handful of snow. Will watched it trickle through the tiny, green-gloved fingers. It fluttered through the air in a scatter of delicate flakes, hanging in the air for a moment before it settled back on to the ground.

And suddenly—he *saw*! He realized what he would have done himself, if he'd been designing the game. Something really brilliant and stylish. Grabbing for the mouse, he clicked, with a triumphant grin. If he could get the snow moving . . .

He scooped the mouse round on its mat and clicked again—and a huge, beautiful arc of snow followed his

53

movement, swirling up into the air and then dropping slowly back. While it was still falling, he scooped again. And again.

In a few seconds, he had raised a complete blizzard, filling the screen with whirling, swirling snowflakes that whited out the sky and almost blotted out the sprites.

But they weren't quite invisible. Through the snow, he could just make out what they were doing. One of them was staggering round in circles and squeaking shrilly, hopelessly confused. That was exactly the sort of thing Will had hoped for. The other one . . .

That wasn't so good. The other sprite had dropped to its knees, with its face close to the ground. Slowly it crawled up to the line of footprints and began to follow them. Annoyingly (*Cheating!* Will thought) the snow didn't fill in the footprints, and the sprite kept its face so low that it could obviously see them.

Not bad. This game designer was certainly original. But that made Will even more determined to win. Furiously, he swirled more snow, scooping it high and scattering it deliberately over the little crawling figure.

It didn't have any effect. The sprite crawled on stoically, towards the left hand edge of the screen and the picture scrolled sideways.

That was when Will saw the tent.

It was a small brown tent, pitched just to one side of the trail of footprints. The instant he spotted it, he knew it was important. He had to stop the sprite from seeing it.

More snow!

Forgetting about the other sprite, which was still wandering round in circles, squeaking forlornly, Will whirled snow at the crawling figure, sweeping the flakes straight into its face so that it hunched even lower, with its nose almost touching the ground. It obviously hadn't noticed the tent, and Will's hand worked like lightning to make sure it didn't notice. *Click, scoop, swirl* . . . Once the wretched thing had gone away, he'd take a look inside the tent himself.

But it didn't happen like that. Because suddenly, from the right hand side of the screen, a crowd of small black shapes erupted into the picture. Penguins. Will blinked at them.

Penguins?

They launched themselves at the confused sprite, the one he had abandoned, bouncing forward to peck at its clothing. Will almost laughed out loud. How could *penguins* do anything deadly?

Then one of them tweaked at the sprite's padded mitten, pulling it off and tossing it away. It sank into the snow, disappearing instantly, and a second penguin dived for the other glove. That didn't look very dangerous. But Will went on watching, still clicking snow at the crawling sprite.

The penguins bounced again and the little explorer waved its hands at them uselessly. Will noticed that its fingers were changing colour. Turning red, then blue, then white. And then black.

Frostbite! Oh, yes! A gold star for the designer! Will grinned as, one by one, the black fingers cracked across and started to tumble to the ground like pieces of glass. Was this a clue? Could he use frostbite as a weapon?

Before he could work out how, the frostbitten sprite let out a loud, piercing squeak, followed by a flurry of shorter ones. And the crawling figure stopped — as though the squeaks meant something. Sitting back on its heels, it looked round.

And saw the tent.

Hey! Not fair! Will was angry. He'd worked hard at that snowstorm and it had all been for nothing. He might just as well have let the wretched sprite go where it wanted in the first place.

But there was no time to argue. The sprite was crawling straight for the tent and the picture was scrolling, to take them inside. Snow and penguins disappeared, and the screen filled up with clutter.

An oil lamp hung from the ridge pole of the tent and there were two heavy, old-fashioned camp beds, one on each side. Between them stood a camping stove and a set of billycans, and along the back several big wooden boxes were stacked up. They were lashed together with thick brown rope, and words were stencilled on their sides. SUPPLIES. BASE CAMP ONE.

Which bits of clutter were important? The sprite was obviously searching for something, but what? Will frowned. He'd just have to attack and hope for the best. Sliding the mouse forward, he clicked on a billycan.

Yes! That was right! The billycan whooshed up into the air, changing into an arrow as it headed across the tent. The sprite darted sideways, out of range, and the arrow buried its point in one of the boxes.

Got it! But he'd have to aim better. How about the stove this time?

The stove changed into an axe, but the sprite just managed to avoid it. Then Will tried the left hand camp bed. It rolled up into a spiked cannonball, but that missed too.

The sprite dodged and ducked, avoiding all Will's missiles somehow. Gradually it made its way across the tent, to the boxes at the back, and Will hunted round for another weapon.

But he knew that would be too slow as well. It was the sprite's dodging that kept defeating him. It kept diving out of the way, after the weapons were thrown, and unless he could overcome that, he'd never get rid of it. The little figure had reached the boxes now, and it was stretching out its hands towards the thick, brown rope that tied them together.

The rope —

Danger! said that eerie sixth sense in Will's head. *Danger!* Suddenly he was desperate to beat the sprite at once. He felt as though he hadn't got much time left.

The rope came tumbling off, falling on to the floor in an awkward brown tangle, and Will sent his mouse racing for the best weapon in the tent—the oil lamp. As he got ready to click, he was thinking at double speed.

He'd missed the sprite so far, because it was too good at dodging. If he was ever going to beat it, he would have to anticipate what it would do. People usually dodged to the left, didn't they? If the game designer was as clever as he seemed to be . . .

Will took a deep breath and gambled. He clicked on the oil lamp and it changed into a flaming torch, heading straight for the sprite as it bent to pick up the rope. Instantly—just *before* the sprite dodged—Will knocked the torch sideways.

It swept to the right, exactly matching the little sprite's leap to the left. And that was it. There was a thud and a great sheet of flame, and the whole picture disappeared as bright letters flashed in the top corner.

Well done. 200 points.

Well done? Will sat back in his chair, letting the mouse fall on to its mat. If he'd done well—why did he feel so unsatisfied?

The only useful thing he'd done was throw the lamp. Apart from that, he might just as well have been watching a television. Everything else had been a waste of time. He felt as though the game wasn't really meant for him at all—as though the sprites were the real players.

But that was ridiculous.

He jabbed at the keyboard, trying to go on, but it was no use, of course. That was the most annoying thing of all. Just when you got going, the thing cut out, leaving you high and dry. He wouldn't be able to have a go at the next level until Wednesday.

Stupid game. He turned off and stood up, stretching. The more he thought about it, the more frustrating and puzzling it seemed. But he wasn't going to let it beat him. He was going to crack it, the way he'd told his father he would.

But he wouldn't say anything to him yet. Not until he'd worked out what was going on.

Chapter 10

SORRY, MIRIAM, YOU'RE DEAD . . .

The stone letters formed in the air, across the flames that were eating up the tent. Miriam stood staring at them, trying to ignore the thought that was forming in her mind. But it wouldn't go away.

Someone had been watching her.

That last missile — the flaming torch — hadn't hit her by accident. Or by bad luck. There was someone in the game who was working out what she would do next. When that flaming torch flew at her, someone had *guessed* which way she was going to dodge.

The pictures faded from her helmet and she stood gazing into the blank screens, putting off the moment when she would have to undo the straps.

The door opened. 'Miriam?'

Slowly, she pulled the helmet off. Hesketh was standing in the doorway, looking at her. But she had no way of telling what he was thinking. His heavy face was expressionless.

'Someone was watching me,' she said.

His face didn't change. '*I* was watching you. Or at least, I was monitoring the game, in various ways. I don't actually sit and stare at a picture.'

'I don't mean you,' Miriam said, impatiently. 'Not unless you interfere with what happens.'

'No one interferes. It's just you and Stuart. And the software.'

'It can't have been Stuart,' Miriam said, slowly. 'I would have seen him, wouldn't I? And anyway, he was outside, fighting killer penguins. I only saw the tent because he shouted and made me look up. The person I'm talking about was *inside*, throwing things. Someone invisible.'

Hesketh smiled. 'There wasn't anyone else.'

'Yes, there *was*! There was someone—' Miriam swallowed, stopped and started again. 'Someone who knew which way I was going to move. *Before I did it.*'

Hesketh's smile disappeared and he was suddenly very still. 'It's not a game like chess,' he said quietly. 'You have to understand that. It's very powerful. Your body goes into battle alert when you're playing, ready to see an enemy behind every bush. You imagine things.'

'I didn't imagine it.' Miriam was still gripping the helmet in both hands, not noticing that he'd picked up the case. Instead of answering, he took her hands and opened the fingers, one by one, until the helmet dropped into the right place.

'Don't fight it,' he said, very softly, gripping her fingers. 'Just go with the game. And trust me.'

Miriam stared down at his hand, cupped round hers, almost swamping it. A heavy, square thumb and a battery of knuckles. Tough and old and very, very solid. *Trust me.*

She wanted to. But she wasn't going to lie to herself so that she could do it. When that flaming torch had aimed itself at her, and then changed direction, at the very moment she dodged, she'd known there was someone trying to knock her out of the game. That had been real. Whatever 'real' meant.

She drew her hand away, and slipped it into her pocket. 'Well,' she said lightly. 'It's all very exciting. I'm looking forward to playing on Wednesday.'

Then she walked out of the building, with her bag in her hand and her head held high.

But she was shaken. As she climbed on to the bus and showed her ticket, her fingers were trembling, and she was glad to sink down into the seat. Her whole brain was jangling with arguments and memories, and she buried her face in her hands, trying to get a grip of herself.

There couldn't be anyone else in the game. She was just being hysterical. After all, she didn't really know how the

60

equipment worked. Maybe it had some way of sensing what she was going to do. Or maybe the whole thing had just been a coincidence.

She couldn't quite explain it all away, but she tried. By the time she reached the towpath, she was telling herself firmly that Hesketh had to be right. Of course he was right. And if he wasn't—what did it matter anyway? She was only playing a game. Everything would be all right if she just kept *calm*. She stepped on to the boat and walked down into the cabin, with her face fixed in a bright, stiff smile.

And Laura took one look at her and shrieked.

'What's up with *you*? You're grinning like a waxwork.'

It was the last straw. Miriam's self-control snapped, and she did what she had wanted to do all along, ever since the flaming torch swerved sideways.

She yelled.

'It's none of your business what I look like! Why don't you leave me alone, you snoopy old hag? Poke, poke, poke! It's a wonder your nose isn't eight metres long. It's a wonder it doesn't get stuck in the *keyhole*!'

Then she stormed straight through into her own cabin, banging the door shut behind her.

She should have known that it wouldn't end there. Laura had been struck dumb all right. Wonderfully, extraordinarily dumb. But it couldn't last. After a few minutes, Miriam heard the noise of the television starting up in the living cabin. And then—presumably when Rachel and Joe were settled in front of it—her door opened slowly.

'Go away!' she said.

That didn't make any difference, of course. The door opened wider, and Laura slipped into the room. For a second or two she stood in the doorway, quite silent, staring at Miriam. Then she came in, closing the door after her, and sat down on Rachel's bunk.

'You've never shouted at me before,' she said. 'Not like that.'

61

Her voice was very soft, and she looked paler than usual, as if she were shaken too. *Good!* Miriam thought.

'You shouldn't go on at me,' she said gruffly. 'There's no privacy. You're always watching me.'

'Well, I can't ignore you, can I?' Laura began. 'And I was concerned—'

Miriam snorted. It was such a Laura word. *Concerned.* Laura was always *concerned* about other people's *feelings*. In a moment she'd start up about being *open* and *honest*, and *sharing things*—as if life were a bag of toffees.

As if no invisible, inexplicable hand ever darted into the bag and snatched away a toffee from under your nose.

Miriam closed her eyes and waited for the rest of the performance. But it didn't come. Laura didn't say a word. She simply sat there, waiting, until Miriam couldn't stand the silence any more and opened her eyes again.

Then she said, 'We can do that if you like.'

'Do what?' Miriam muttered.

'We can have the sort of conversation we always have. With me being bossy and saying what I think, and you trying to freeze me out. But I'm sick of that. The more we do it, the worse things get. Why don't we talk properly for once?'

Miriam stared at her. Watching how her hands clenched in her lap, and how her throat moved when she swallowed.

Laura faltered and looked down. 'I'm sorry I jumped on you when you came in. I know I open my mouth first and think later. But when you walked through that door, I could see there was something wrong. And I just felt—'

'I was *smiling*, for heaven's sake!'

'Oh, but I know that smile.' Laura's mouth twisted. 'I ought to. It's the way you smiled when you were three. When you heard I was going to marry your father. Your making-the-best-of-a-bad-job smile.'

She laughed, a nervous, uncertain laugh, and Miriam could see what it had cost her to speak like that. For a moment she'd had to stop pretending that they were all one big, happy family. Her hands twisted together even more tightly and she looked up, waiting for an answer.

Miriam couldn't bear it. It was like being asked for sympathy—and she didn't want to be sympathetic. She didn't want to be friendly and soften up and . . . and *let Laura in*. Rearing up on the bed, she hissed at her, spitting out the words.

'And I have made the best of a bad job! I do my share of the chores. I don't make a fuss when you pry into my life. Or scream when you shriek and giggle like a fool. I leave you alone. I just wish you'd do the same for me. *Why don't you stop watching?*'

The moment she'd said it, she knew it was too much. But she couldn't unsay the words, because they were true. Laura stood up and brushed savagely at the blanket fluff on her skirt.

'Watching?' she said bitterly. 'That's all you see, isn't it? You think I'm some kind of spy. Don't you understand —?'

She stopped and took a long, deep breath, staring across the cabin. Miriam avoided her eyes and, at last, she turned towards the door.

'I don't think this is doing either of us any good,' she muttered. 'I'm going to take Joe and Rachel for a walk. And we'd better try and forget everything that's been said.'

The door opened and then closed again and, for a moment, there were yells in the living cabin.

'Mum! I wanted to see the rest of that programme!'

'I'm not going for a walk without Miriam! She always — '

Then the outside door banged and the shouts died away, accompanied by the sound of footsteps along the towpath. Slowly, Miriam stood up and walked out of her cabin, drawing long, deep breaths. She filled up the electric kettle and plugged it in.

But somehow the cup of coffee she made didn't warm her up as much as she hoped. Now that Laura had gone, the air in the boat seemed flat and dusty. And the river lapped greyly against the sides of the boat.

Glock, glock, glock.

K & K: ELECTRONIC MEMO
HESKETH BARRINGTON TO JOHN SHELLEY
PRIORITY: NORMAL

We gave them an exciting time today and results were as predicted. Ordinary excitement does not interfere with the stress monitor. Next time we'll give Subject B something a bit special, to put the screws on. But he should be fine. (Bar a heart attack or two.)

K & K: ELECTRONIC MEMO
JOHN SHELLEY TO HESKETH BARRINGTON
PRIORITY: URGENT

There's no time for heart attacks. Or jokes. Can't you speed things up a bit? If you can get through in another two weeks, we could still meet our original schedule, in spite of the game trauma scare.

You'd do yourself a lot of good if you helped us meet that schedule.

Chapter 11

Why don't you stop watching? The words kept echoing in Miriam's ears. Because suddenly Laura was being very careful *not* to watch. Looking out of the window, or down at the newspaper, or anywhere to stop their eyes meeting. Choosing her words carefully so that nothing sounded like a question.

But that only made things worse, because they couldn't stop being conscious of each other. The more Laura avoided her, the more Miriam felt watched, not by eyes, but in a hundred other ways. Every time she made a movement — every time she took a breath — she could feel the sound travelling to Laura's ears, and she found herself listening for Laura's movements in the same way. They were both painfully, electrically, aware.

Miriam saw her father notice it too. He didn't say anything, but his eyes followed them miserably as they avoided each other. More staring. Whenever Miriam turned round, he seemed to glance away quickly, and whenever she spoke to Laura she could feel him listening.

There was no escape. First there'd been the invisible watcher, in the game, and now there were eyes everywhere. Miriam felt huge and awkward, as though she'd been stuck up on a stage for everyone to goggle at. There didn't seem to be anywhere for her to hide.

She found herself glancing backwards all the time. Looking over her shoulder as she walked down the towpath. Turning round when she was running up the road to school. Staring up and down the cafeteria queue at lunchtime, in case someone was watching behind her back. Every time she turned round, she expected to see — eyes.

She told herself that it didn't matter. It was just a silly habit, because of what had happened in the game. If she ignored it until they played again, on Wednesday, the whole thing would probably sort itself out. So she looked as cheerful as she could, and forced herself to behave normally, grinning at Debbie's pathetic jokes and her tales about Pete, the red-haired boy. She made herself pay attention in class, and put up her hand as usual. She even joined in the gossip and giggles at break, pretending she cared. It was a very good performance.

But she didn't keep it up quite long enough. On Wednesday afternoon, when she thought she was home and dry, she gave herself away. She was rattling out of school, to catch the bus to K & K, and she got caught in a jam at the school gate. There were too many people trying to get through, and they'd all started pushing and shrieking, refusing to give way. Miriam checked her watch, fretting with impatience and peering down the road for the bus.

And then, in the middle of the crush, she felt someone staring.

She didn't know how she knew. She just had a curious feeling of space and quietness behind her, a gap in the middle of all the shoving and yelling. She spun round — and there was Connie, long-legged and casual, draped over the handlebars of her bike. Gazing at Miriam with curious, treacle-brown eyes.

Miriam was consumed with fury. Before she could stop herself, she leaned forward and hissed fiercely.

'Stop it! You're always *staring* at me. Why don't you keep your eyes to yourself?'

Instantly, she knew she'd made a fool of herself. People turned round to look, and there were some sniggers from behind as the crowd pushed forward. They knew that Connie had once been Miriam's best friend, and that she wasn't any more, and they were hoping for a nice, juicy argument. Maybe even a fight.

But Connie just smiled her easy, untroubled smile, and spread her hands out, disclaiming any responsibility. Then she swung herself gracefully on to the bike and swooped out through the gates as the crush cleared. Stalking after her, Miriam avoided everyone's eyes, and headed for the bus stop.

The bus was early — Christine Riley's car was still on the Ring Road when it flashed past — and Miriam jumped on to it thankfully, eager to be at K & K and get started. She wasn't going to wait for Stuart. She was going to race in and begin, as quickly as she could. Once she'd played again, she would get rid of this stupid, paranoid feeling of being spied on. And anyway, she needed to get ahead and get some points.

When she got off the bus, she ran all the way to K & K, and she didn't waste any time talking to Hesketh. As soon as she could manage it, she was alone in the game room, pulling on her helmet.

She found herself alone in the rainbow room. There was no sign of Stuart. Swooping across to the glass case, she opened the map and slammed her hand down on to the wide violet shape in the very centre. If she could get into Africa before Stuart appeared, maybe he wouldn't be able to follow her at all. Then she would have the whole level to herself. She gazed down at the map, waiting to see what she would have to find.

Two long, narrow shapes whirled up towards her, light flashing from their blades. Their points pierced the air as they crossed and uncrossed, weaving patterns in front of her and making wide extravagant flourishes. Then the room began to spin, and she closed her eyes.

Here we go . . .

But, while they were still shut, she heard Stuart's voice.

'What are you up to?' He sounded angry. 'Why didn't you wait for me?'

Without answering, she opened her eyes. Straight ahead, through the violet door, she could see green. A mass of different greens, dappled one on another, rustled in a luminous twilight, shivering with a constant, whispering motion.

But she couldn't see much of them, because there was a grey shape standing four-square in front of the door. A furious shape. Stuart had his head flung back and his shoulders set aggressively.

'D'you think you're playing this game on your own?' he hissed.

Miriam shrugged. 'Aren't we playing against each other? Trying to get the best score?'

'We still ought to start level, or it's not fair.'

'We are level.' Miriam glided towards him. 'You just missed choosing the continent, and what does that matter? We're bound to have to visit them all in the end.'

'But I don't know what we're looking for!' Stuart said.

His voice went suddenly shrill, and Miriam could see him in her mind. His scrawny face with its pop-eyes and steamed-up glasses. Why was he fussing so much when they could be getting on with the game?

'We're looking for swords,' she said. 'OK? Now stop wasting time.'

'I'm *not* wasting time. I want to go back to the map and see for myself. You can't just — '

But Miriam had had enough. She sidestepped neatly past him, through the door. Trying to stop her, Stuart jumped back, over-balanced, and crossed the threshold at the same moment. They were both in the jungle.

Immediately, the door swung shut and the dappled green closed round them. They were standing on the bank of a wide, slow river, where sunbathing crocodiles lay in an ungainly sprawl and insects hummed over the surface of the water. A wall of creepers hung down on their left, screening the deeper jungle beyond.

Miriam glanced at Stuart — and had to choke to stop herself laughing. He looked about seventy, with a weathered face and a drooping white moustache. His eyes were shaded by a huge, old-fashioned pith helmet, and he was wearing a khaki shirt, with a pair of binoculars hanging round his neck.

69

But the funniest things were his legs. They were skinny and hairy, with very knobbly knees, and he was wearing baggy shorts and enormous walking boots.

'I can't——' She spluttered for a moment and then gave in and laughed out loud. 'You look *hilarious!*'

'You're not exactly beautiful yourself.' Stuart turned away and began to study the wall of creepers, hunting for a way through.

Walking up to the river bank, Miriam stared down into the water. The reflection that gazed back at her looked at least as funny as Stuart. It had the same pith helmet and the same baggy shorts, but the hair was grey, pulled into a tight little bun, and there was a butterfly net strapped to its back, in place of Stuart's binoculars. The Complete Lady Explorer. She grinned.

As though she had given a signal, the crocodiles raised their ugly heads, one by one, and opened their mouths to show rows of gleaming teeth.

Miriam took a step backwards. 'Better get away from here. Unless you want to know what it's like inside a crocodile.'

'I'll leave that to you,' Stuart said sourly.

He didn't wait for an answer. Instead, he marched straight at the wall of creepers, and they parted to let him through. Miriam heard the sound of feet on a hard floor, and she realized that he was taking real steps. Stamping on that floor — wherever it was — to relieve his feelings.

She glided after him and the creepers rustled as she walked between them, into the warm green shadows behind.

Quietness closed round her. The noise of the river died away, and there was no sound from the moving creepers or the animals on the river bank. Everything was dark and silent, as though they had stepped into an empty, shuttered hall.

Miriam looked nervously from side to side, blinded by the shadows. Everything was shadowy, but little dots of light

70

flickered briefly between the trees. Bright points of light, like eyes blinking from behind the creepers. Miriam's pulse skipped, and her heart thudded faster for a moment.

Then she remembered what Hesketh had said. *Your body goes into battle alert.* Deliberately, she relaxed her muscles, taking long, deep breaths.

As her eyes grew used to the gloom, she began to look round properly. Giant trees stretched up like pillars towards the jungle canopy, impossibly high above. Great vines hung motionless, climbing towards the sky, and the forest floor was littered with dead leaves and branches. Everything was dim and tall and quiet. And very still. Apart from the two of them, turning round to gaze, there was no movement anywhere.

Then, very gently, something tickled the back of Miriam's hand.

The sensation itself was nothing. Left to herself, she would barely have noticed it, but Stuart made her notice. Because he stopped moving. Suddenly he was completely — unnaturally — still, staring towards her hand. The comic, explorer's face was expressionless, but his whole body was rigid, and the rasping of his breath unsettled the shadowy silence.

Miriam looked down. She saw something moving jerkily across her skin. A little shape that scuttled, then paused for an instant and then moved again, tickling, almost imperceptibly, as it went.

Crawling from her fingers towards her wrist was a small, black spider.

Chapter 12

'Oh, yes!'

Will was getting to recognize the chances. The little oddities that meant there was going to be some action. Until now, it had just been squeaking and more squeaking, first in the room with the doors and then in the jungle. *Squeak, squeak, squeak.*

Once they were through the door, the sprites looked as silly as they sounded. Intrepid Victorian Naturalists, blundering into the Dark Continent. This time one of them was female, a tough old bird with a butterfly net. Deadlier than the male? Probably. The game was full of corny old clichés.

Will grinned as the explorers crashed through the creepers into the jungle darkness. He'd really enjoy polishing off those two imperialists. If the game ever got going properly.

It did, but not in the way he'd been expecting. There was no invasion of leaping lions, no surge of ravening tigers out of the bushes. Instead, all of a sudden, the whole screen grew very, very still.

And the he-explorer froze completely.

That was the only word for it. Normally the two sprites were always moving about. Nodding, or walking, or waving their arms. And squeaking, of course. But this was quite different. After a single, startled jerk, the he-explorer was absolutely, rigidly still, and completely silent. It seemed to be staring towards the other sprite, gazing as if it were bewitched, at the she-explorer's hand.

Leaning forward, Will could just make out a small black dot, moving very slowly across that hand. He peered at the dot, trying to see what it was, but while he was still puzzling, the she-explorer flicked its arm. The black speck flew away, across the clearing. For a split second it was in the air, and then it was lost in the tangled green of the jungle.

But in that split second, Will caught a single clear glimpse of it, outlined against a patch of pale leaves. He could hardly believe his eyes.

A *spider?*

He almost laughed out loud. The Intrepid Naturalist was scared of spiders? That was a really comic touch. Subtle. Well, it was going to get lots more spiders, if he could arrange it. That one hadn't been put into the game for nothing. It was a hint.

Leaning forward, Will began to search the background, studying every inch of the screen. Somewhere there must be spiders, hidden for him to find. On the jungle floor maybe, or high in the trees. Or in the centre of the parasitic plants that clung half-way up the tree trunks. There *had* to be more spiders.

But the sprites began to push their way through the jungle, and he still hadn't found any. He was starting to wonder whether the spider had been a red herring, when he realized what he was doing wrong.

He was expecting things to be too easy.

When he played before, things hadn't been handed to him. Weapons hadn't been lying around, ready to be picked up. He'd had to see through the disguises that hid the weapons before he could do anything.

So how had the spiders been disguised?

His eyes raced over the screen again, but this time he was looking at everything in a different way. He wasn't hunting for real spiders, he was searching for things that *looked like* spiders. Tangled clumps of creeper. Little heaps of leaves on the ground. Strange, spiky flowers nestled in the centre of the parasitic bromeliads.

And they jumped out at him from every side. The jungle was full of them. He picked a cluster of vine stems half-way up a tree and sent his arrow swooping towards them. *Click.*

73

It worked like magic. The stems twisted and wriggled — and there was a fat spider, as big as the explorers' heads. Exactly the same size as the original cluster of stems. It dropped from the vines on a long thread and began to spin a web.

Oh, no you don't, thought Will. *I need you.* He clicked again, and the spider went flying across the clearing, towards the explorers.

Take that!

It was perfect. *Squeak, squeak, squeak, SQUEAK!* The he-explorer froze again, its arms close to its sides and its body motionless, and the she-explorer began to run round in circles, trying to flick the spider away.

Great. Will raced into action. He sent his arrow dancing all over the screen and spiders materialized from nowhere, spinning their way out of every shadow. After a moment or two, they were crawling all over the screen, dropping out of the trees in front of the explorers and climbing up their legs.

The she-explorer carried on like a maniac, flicking the little black bodies away and stamping on the ones underfoot. For a second, Will just watched, admiring the bright green SPLAT! the spiders made when they burst. Then he remembered the he-explorer. That was the one the spiders were meant for. What was it doing?

It was very disappointing. Will had expected wonderful, dramatic terror. He'd hoped it would turn red and white with shock. He wanted to hear it scream and see its hair stand on end. But nothing like that happened. The sprite just stayed still and silent. OK, so maybe it was paralysed with fear. Maybe it was so petrified it couldn't *breathe.* But that was *boring.* Will wanted more than that.

He looked round the screen, frowning hard. What he wanted was . . . Yes! There!

Immediately above the he-explorer's head was a tight, black tangle of creepers. Will slid his little red arrow towards it. That was just what he wanted, and it was in exactly the right place.

Click!

The creepers wriggled, twisted, and turned into a neat, chunky spider with eight hairy legs. And it didn't waste time. As soon as it was a spider, it began to spin, letting itself down slowly, very slowly, towards the he-explorer's head. Will grinned. It couldn't have been better. If the he-explorer didn't move, the spider was going to land on the very tip of its nose. *That* ought to fix it!

Down came the spider, invisible from below until the very last moment. Then —

But what happened wasn't at all like the terror Will had expected. Instead of dramatic screams and hair on end, there was one shrill squeak from the he-explorer. Then it began to raise its hands towards its head. Very slowly, as though the movement were an enormous effort. And, when the hands were half-way there, suspended in mid-air —

It disappeared.

Will stared at the screen. What was that for? He'd been brilliant. Intelligent and fast and inventive. Now he wanted points and flashing lights and a fanfare of trumpets. But there was nothing. What did the game think it was doing?

For a second, he was sick of the whole thing. His hand moved towards the switch, to turn it off.

Then he noticed what the she-explorer was up to. Now it was alone, it had stopped squeaking, and it wasn't loitering around any more. Instead, with a steady determination, it was setting off into the jungle, trampling the spiders underfoot as though they weren't there.

Oh no, you don't! Will thought. He wasn't going to let this one get away. If it didn't take any notice of ordinary spiders, maybe the game would give him something better. Something it *couldn't* trample on.

He scanned the screen for a third time. Looking for a much, much bigger tangle of stems.

75

Chapter 13

Zap! One moment Stuart was there, and the next he wasn't. He had vanished completely.

Miriam blinked and looked round. What had happened? Had a spider bitten him? Had there been a power cut at his house? Or had he just switched off because he didn't like spiders?

That was a possibility. There were certainly enough of the wretched things about. They were so thick on the ground that she couldn't move without stepping on one or two, and squirting herself with bright green goo. If Stuart really *was* scared of spiders, he must have been going crazy.

Well, she wasn't going to let them put her off. If she went on standing around in this clearing, she would never get anywhere. It was time to head into the jungle, to hunt for the swords she was supposed to be finding. She took a couple of squelchy, green steps to the edge of the clearing.

And then she saw the giant spider.

It seemed to appear out of nowhere. One moment, there was nothing ahead of her except a huge tangle of creepers, as high as a house, and the next moment — she was facing a monster.

A vast, ugly spider towered over her, its bowed, hairy legs longer than her whole body. It had begun to spin a web, and it was hanging on to the sticky threads, vibrating gently, a vast, disgusting blob. The shock of its appearance made Miriam catch her breath.

Then she thought — *Great!*

In real life, she would have been mad not to run away from a spider like that. But this wasn't real life. This was a game, and the way to win was to go straight into danger. To meet the enemies that appeared, and defeat them.

It was a pity she didn't have a weapon, but she would have to use what she did have. Gathering her wits, she felt her body grow tense and alert. Then she launched herself forward until the spider was towering over her, reaching out its jointed, hairy legs towards her face. Drawing back her right fist, she smashed out at the nearest leg, as hard as she could.

The force of the punch nearly sent her flying. She had put her whole body behind it, forgetting that she wasn't really going to hit anything solid. All she felt, as the blow connected, was the pressure from the inflated pads in her glove and she staggered and almost fell.

But that didn't matter. Not next to the wonderful, dramatic effect of her punch. The spider gave a loud, shrill squeal and the leg she had punched snapped in half with a satisfying crack.

Instantly, the spider sent a long, sticky strand of web-thread snaking down towards her. But Miriam had been expecting some kind of retaliation, and she was ready. She darted sideways, and the thread looped round the tree next to her, pulling tight and sticking fast. If she had stayed still, she would have been trapped.

But she wasn't trapped.

And she wasn't going to be. She was going to have a wonderful battle with the spider—and she was going to win!

From the top joint of the severed leg, a thick glob of green slime dripped down on to the back of her right hand. Brushing it away impatiently, she bunched her fingers into a fist again and struck out at a second leg.

Crack!

With another splatter of green slime, the second leg snapped. This time, the spider reacted faster, and the web-thread came flashing across in front of Miriam's face. But she was even quicker, flinging herself out of its way.

She was grinning. There was no need to worry about the spider's feelings. No need to fret that it might come from an endangered species, or be crucial to the ecology of the jungle. It was *made* to be her enemy, and there was no need to do anything except smash it!

As she clenched her fist for a third time, it felt stiff and awkward. The pads inside the Game Glove had inflated, making it harder to bend her fingers. Glancing down at the hand, she saw that it looked swollen, and the skin was covered with a rash of red spots.

What did that mean? Was the green slime poisonous? Probably. In that case, she'd have to get a move on, before she dropped down dead.

Somewhere in the distance, a steady drumming had started up, its vibrations filling the air around her. And under the drumming, almost too faint to hear, was a soft, rhythmic chant.

. . . *min-na, min-na, min-na* . . .

It was just faster than her pulsebeat and her heart seemed to speed up in sympathy, pumping more adrenalin round her body.

. . . *min-na, min-na, min-na* . . .

Let the poison do its worst! She didn't feel ready to die. She felt *alive*. Swinging her fist again, she smashed the spider's third leg, and this time she saw it totter on its web. That was it! One more blow and it would come tumbling down. Then she could break through its web and go on, into the jungle.

The web thread flicked her hand as it swished past this time, and her fingers felt more and more swollen. She hadn't got long. But she was determined to win. She wasn't going to let the poison kill her before she found the swords. Faster! She drew back her hand to punch again.

And then, for the first time, she saw the other web, hanging above the spider she was fighting. It was high in the treetops, but the bottom was attached to the web she was shaking with her punches. And hanging from it was a curious, distorted creature.

Another spider? Miriam wasn't sure. It was too high in the shadows for her to make out any details, but she had a vague impression of something deformed. Something jagged and harsh and threatening. With a shudder, she stopped and stared up at it.

What would happen when she smashed through the bottom web? Would that horrible thing at the top fall straight on to her head? Maybe it was doubly poisonous, a final enemy to kill her off. Maybe—

But there was no time to dither. The wounded spider sent another sticky thread lashing towards her, and the poisonous slime dripped again. In a few moments, she would probably be dead anyway.

Bunching her fist, she swung, with all her force, at the giant, wounded spider. This time, she aimed not at a leg but at the soft, vibrating abdomen that swung above her head.

BLEUGGHH!

The spider split open, with a great gush of slime, and its web ripped across, tearing into tatters. Miriam jumped back, trying to get clear before the upper web tumbled down on top of her.

But it didn't tumble. It just sagged slightly, staying out of reach but coming low enough for her to get a better view of the creature squatting in the middle. She frowned up at it.

It had too few legs. Only four. And no abdomen. And . . .

And then she realized. The thing wasn't a spider. It wasn't alive at all. It was made out of two blades, crossed to look like four legs.

Sword-blades!

For a moment she actually forgot that she was in a game. Reaching out, she grabbed at one of the creepers beside her, meaning to climb up it.

It fizzed and disappeared in her hands, and she shook her head impatiently. Stupid! She should have known that climbing was impossible. There had to be some other way of reaching the swords. But what? If she couldn't climb, and she couldn't pull down the creepers, that only left—

Of course! The sticky web-thread!

Ripping at the broken web in front of her, she grabbed a handful of strands and pressed them together. They stuck to each other, magically twisting themselves into a long, thin rope.

Her heart beat faster, and the drumming and chanting speeded up to match it.

. . . *min-na, min-na, min-na* . . .

The glove was very tight now, and uncomfortable when she bent her fingers, but she forced herself to hold on to the rope. Gathering it into a bundle, she threw it, as hard as she could. It flew up into the air, crashing against the swords. One end stuck to them, and the other came tumbling down again, straight into her hands.

She clutched it hard, and pulled.

With a great crash, the swords toppled out of the web, to fall at her feet. As she bent to pick them up, the drumming accelerated and there was a deafening, triumphant fanfare of trumpets. Flaming, scarlet shapes flashed in front of her eyes.

CONGRATULATIONS, MIRIAM!
2000 POINTS!

The swords glittered golden in her hands, and she raised them above her head, holding them high as the jungle began to spin and the drums and trumpets swelled in an almost unbearable crescendo.

And then it was all over. Quite suddenly. The music stopped, the Game Glove loosened and the helmet screens went dead.

For a second, she stood like that, catching her breath. Then she heard the door opening and, slowly, she slid the helmet off her head. Hesketh was standing in the doorway staring at her.

'Well?' he said.

It wasn't really a question. She could see that he knew, exactly, how she felt. He must be able to tell from her eyes, and from the stupid, uncontrolled grin that spread across her face.

'Not bad,' she said, as casually as she could.

But it was no use trying to play it down. The moment she'd said the words, she started to laugh at the ridiculous inadequacy of them. And Hesketh laughed too, opening his mouth like a red cavern. Showing glittering golden teeth.

'You like my spiders?'

He reached his huge hands towards her, the fingers curved threateningly, and gold glittered there too, flashing from a signet ring. For an instant, as he towered in the doorway, he looked utterly splendid and dangerous. A wizard who had conjured the whole game — the whole New World — out of thin air. If he had flicked his fingers and said that all the talk of programming and silicon chips was just a blind, to hide his magic, Miriam would have believed him absolutely.

Because the power was in *him*. By crooking his little finger, or raising his eyebrows, he could call continents into being, or summon up tidal waves to drown them. The sun would blaze when he flashed his golden teeth, and the sky would grow black and thunderous when he roared with the cavern of his mouth.

He stared down at her. 'Were you afraid?'

Go on, challenged his eyes. *Put it into words. Tell me how you felt.* But Miriam knew she couldn't. There were no words at all. Nothing she could say. Only —

'POW!'

She yelled it at the top of her voice, swinging her fist, and the Game Glove almost caught the wriggling tips of Hesketh's huge, enchanter's fingers.

He laughed again, and grabbed the glove to unfasten it, but that didn't break the spell. As they walked through the big Research and Development room, and down the middle of the building, Miriam was still moving in an irrational, magic world.

The huge glass walls of the atrium glittered like crystal cliffs on either side of her. The giant creepers that festooned the space seemed conjured up by spells. She was passing through an enchanted cavern, accompanying a sorcerer.

All the way home, she was in a golden daze, staring through the window of the bus without seeing anything. And every time she thought *Africa*, a laugh welled up inside her, and she had to struggle to keep silent.

Even Laura couldn't break her triumph. Miriam swept on to the boat with a cheerful smile, beaming at everyone.

'Had a good day?'

'*Not* one of the best,' Laura said drily.

Miriam took in the situation at a glance. Rachel was curled up in a corner, sulking about something, and Joe was playing a very messy game with plastic bricks and a lump of raw, grey pastry.

Miriam beamed again. 'Come on, you two. How about some fishing?'

'Yeah!'

'Great!'

They were on their feet at once, and Miriam carried them off, enjoying the startled look on Laura's face. When their father came walking along the towpath, the three of them were sitting on the roof of the boat, dangling bits of string into the water.

He smiled. 'Hallo.'

Only Miriam looked up. Joe and Rachel were watching their string with rapt, breathless attention. They didn't seem to have noticed their father at all.

He smiled. 'Training them to hunt for themselves are you?' he murmured. 'Well done, Minnow.'

Minnow. He never called her that when anyone else was around, but it didn't seem strange to Miriam at that moment. Joe and Rachel were so silent that she had almost forgotten they were there. And they weren't listening, anyway.

But that didn't mean they hadn't heard. Their father's voice had been just too loud, and Rachel looked up suddenly.

'Minnow?' she said. Swinging round, she tugged at Miriam's hair. 'Minnow *Mouse!*'

Miriam's golden glow began to drain away. She didn't know why. Except that — there was something odd about that name. Something she ought to have remembered . . .

'Minnow!' Rachel shrieked again.

'Shut up,' Miriam said.

Her father looked quizzically at her. 'Don't you like being called that?'

'I — ' she blinked. Forced herself to smile back. 'Of course I do. It's just — I don't like anyone else to say it.'

Didn't he know it was private and special? Something uneasy began to nag at the back of her mind. To stop it, she spoke again, more sharply than she meant to.

'You're not to tell Laura. I don't want *Laura* calling me that.'

The moment she'd said it, she knew it was quite wrong. The thing that was bothering her had nothing to do with Laura. But, by then, it was too late to take the words back. Her father looked down at her, taking in the way she sat and the tone of her voice, but he didn't say anything else. Just smiled his tender, meek smile and went into the cabin, to change out of his one good suit.

Miriam stared at the grey, rippled water and trawled through her mind. *Minnow.*

Joe snuggled up against her side. Like an echo, he whispered in her ear. 'Minnow. Minnow, minnow, minnow . . .'

And suddenly she was back in the shadowy dungeon, with her hand between the jagged teeth. She was plunging through the jungle, smashing spiders' webs. And the faint, insistent voices were whispering in her ear.

. . . *min-na, min-na, min-na . . . min-now, min-now, min-now . . .*

'Stop it!' she said abruptly.

She pushed Joe away and pulled in her fishing line, winding it up tight.

K & K: ELECTRONIC MEMO
HESKETH BARRINGTON TO JOHN SHELLEY
PRIORITY: NORMAL

It works! The damn thing works like a dream! Just wait until you see my charts of the stress monitor readings. [attached] The line shoots straight up and then — BANG! Total cutout.

Subject B seems to be fine. See Christine Riley's observer's report. [attached] His attachment to the game isn't damaged. Within ten minutes, he was talking about the next session.

It's looking good for the original schedule.

K & K: ELECTRONIC MEMO
JOHN SHELLEY TO HESKETH BARRINGTON
PRIORITY: NORMAL

Impressive stuff. I've told Promotions and Marketing to keep to their original dates. They're just waiting for your final results and then they'll go into action.

Chapter 14

Minnow...

No! She wouldn't think about it.

She chivvied Rachel and Joe inside and tried to distract herself by chopping cabbage for supper. But it was no use. That unsettling, frightening voice went whispering on in her head.

... min-now, min-now, min-now ...

She couldn't block it out just by doing things. She needed to fill her brain as well as her hands. She needed to talk and talk—and *argue*. So hard that she had no thoughts left over for anything else.

She put down the chopping knife and looked up at Laura, bursting out with the first thing that came into her head.

'So you don't mind Rachel and Joe going fishing? I thought you were against blood sports? Or is that just when they're not useful to you?'

Laura was peeling oranges with a sharp knife, neatly flicking out the skinless sections. 'I don't think *that* sort of fishing counts as a blood sport,' she said vaguely.

But Miriam wasn't going to let her get away with that. She *needed* to argue. 'Oh, great. So fox-hunting's fine as long as they don't catch the fox?'

'No, of course it's not.' Laura put down the knife. 'But that's quite different—'

'I don't see why.'

They were away. And the argument was fast and hard. After a few moments, Miriam saw her father stick his head out of the front cabin. He was frowning anxiously—until he saw how Laura's eyes were sparkling as she argued. When she began hammering the worktop with her fist, he grinned and went back inside to find a jumper.

Laura drove the questions away for a good while. And when they came back—in a slack moment at school —Debbie was there to provide a distraction. Miriam broke into the middle of a story she was telling about Pete.

'OK, so it's funny. But don't you ever *worry* about the things he does? Some of them are pretty cruel.'

Debbie fired up at once. 'Don't be so po-faced. What's wrong with a joke or two?'

'But this Jojo he keeps teasing—he's a person too, isn't he? Don't you think—?'

No, Debbie didn't. She defended Pete much harder than she would ever have defended herself, and Miriam had to keep her wits about her to argue back. Her mind had no chance to wander off, or worry about anything else.

It ought to have worked. It nearly worked. She might even have managed to forget about the chanting voices in the game—if it hadn't been for Connie.

She should never have shouted like that, in the crush at the gate. Anyone but Connie would have been embarrassed afterwards, or made a point of staring even harder, just to tease her, but Connie wasn't like that. She always wanted to understand what had happened. That was one of the reasons their friendship had broken up. She had to *know.*

She was never in a hurry about it though. On Thursday, she didn't take much notice of Miriam at all. She waited for the right moment and it came on Friday, when Mrs Jackson was looking for someone to tidy the Drama cupboard.

Quite casually, Connie put up her hand and said, 'Miriam and I will do it.'

The deftness of it took Miriam's breath away. How could she refuse? Mrs Jackson was already nodding approval, and shaking her head at Debbie, who was trying to volunteer as well.

'I said *two* people, Deborah.' She dropped the key of the Drama cupboard into Miriam's lap. 'If you start straight after lunch, you'll have almost an hour to do it in.'

Connie smiled and ignored Miriam again, until they were on their own in the Drama cupboard, sorting out the tangled heaps of costumes on the floor. And even then she took her time. They'd been there at least ten minutes before she shook out a scarlet cloak and glanced up.

'Well?' she said.

Miriam frowned. 'Well what?'

'Don't you owe me an apology? For yelling at me on Wednesday.'

She stood there waiting for an answer, with the scarlet satin draped over her arm. Miriam scowled at her.

'You stop staring, and I'll stop shouting at you.'

I wasn't staring. That was what Connie was supposed to say. Debs would have yelled it straight away, and probably given her a shove as well. Then they would have had a safe, noisy quarrel.

But Connie just smiled. 'I like staring at you. You're puzzling.'

That caught Miriam off guard. 'Puzzling? Me?'

'At the moment. You keep doing — unexpected things. Like shouting at me, and arguing with Debbie. That's not like you at all.'

Connie turned away to hang up the cloak and Miriam bent down angrily, snatching up a tangle of tights.

'My character's none of your business! And I can't *bear* being watched.'

'I know,' Connie said. She glanced over her shoulder. 'Why not? Guilty conscience?'

'Don't be stupid!'

'Or maybe . . .' There was a slight, unusual hesitation. Then, abruptly, Connie turned round. 'Look, Miriam, I've got the most peculiar feeling about you at the moment. I know you hate people snooping, but — ' She stopped.

That was unusual, too. Miriam tugged at the knot of tights. 'Why don't you spit it out?' she said irritably. 'I know you. You won't give up until you do.'

Connie went pink. 'All right, I will. I think you're in danger. Am I right?'

It wasn't the sort of question Miriam had been expecting, and it caught her off balance. *In trouble*, she could have fended off. But — in danger? She stared down at the floor.

'I don't know what you mean,' she said stiffly.

Connie didn't give way. 'Yes, you do. You're really jumpy. The way you were that time at Primary School — when we broke Laura's mirror. You're frightened of something, aren't you?'

She reached over and took the tights out of Miriam's hands. They were hopelessly knotted together now, twisted round and round each other into a heavy, complicated tangle. Slowly, Connie began to work the ends loose, freeing one leg after another. Letting them drop from the central knot until it drooped in her hands like a monstrous, many-legged spider.

Miriam didn't mean to speak, but she'd had years of telling Connie things, and suddenly she found herself saying, 'What would you do if you felt someone was watching you? Someone who knew — private things about you?'

Connie's eyes were on the knot. Her long white fingers hooked another leg free of the tangle. 'People can't know about you by magic. They have to find out somehow.'

'But what if there's no way they *could* have found out?'

'Then maybe it's just a coincidence. Or a trick.' The knot fell apart suddenly, and Connie looked up and smiled. 'Some people are very good at pretending they know everything.'

'I — ' Miriam's head was starting to buzz. If she didn't get out now, she would end up telling Connie all about everything. Jerkily she pushed the door open. 'I'm sorry, but I've got to go.'

'Please yourself,' Connie scooped up another heap of clothes and turned away. But, as Miriam stepped through the door, she murmured, 'Don't forget, you can always ask.'

'Ask?' Miriam looked back at her. 'Ask who? What?'

'You can ask me,' Connie said steadily. 'If you need anything. I don't laugh, you know. And I'll help you if I can.'

She was trying to make their eyes meet, but Miriam avoided that, deliberately. 'You might help,' she muttered, 'but what about the questions? You've always got questions, haven't you?'

There was a split second's pause. Then Connie said, almost too softly to hear, 'Not if you don't want them. If you really need help, you can ask for it, and there won't be any questions at all. That's a promise.'

This time, Miriam did meet her eyes. They were very dark and steady.

'I . . . thanks.'

That was the only thing to say. Without another word, Miriam stepped outside and shut the door between them.

She knew she could trust Connie's promise. Maybe, one day, she would even need help without questions. But, all the same, she wished that the conversation had never happened. It had started up her thoughts again, and set her thinking about the person who had watched her in the game. Who interfered and knew too much about her.

The person who called her Minnow.

Stuart logged in first that afternoon. When Miriam reached the rainbow room, he was standing with his back to her, hunched over the map. She didn't make a sound to let him know she was there. She just glided up behind him and hissed in his ear.

'What happened to you on Wednesday?'

He whipped round. If he'd had a face, he would have pulled it. Miriam was sure that out there in his home he *was* pulling one. But he didn't say a word. He just reached

90

out and jammed his hand down on the big green patch that was Asia.

'Hang on —'

But it was too late for Miriam to do anything. A circular blur came spinning up towards her, whirling dizzily.

'What's that meant to be?' she muttered.

Stuart's head lifted and turned towards her, but he still didn't say a word.

'Oh, for heaven's sake!' Miriam snapped. 'What's the point of sulking? It's not my fault if the spiders scared you out of the game.'

He spoke then all right. Very distant and cold, as though the words were choking him.

'Who said I was scared? I was fine. If you hadn't made such a fuss, I could have gone on playing.'

'*Me?*' Miriam was righteously indignant. 'What's it got to do with me?'

'You made it look as if I was petrified. Racing round flicking at all those spiders. That's what did it. Hesketh must have pulled me out of the game.'

Miriam stared at him. 'I thought you pulled yourself out. Because of the spiders.'

'I wasn't scared!' Stuart snapped. For a moment he lost control of his voice and it went very shrill.

'Why did you take your helmet off, then?'

The room had begun to spin. Miriam closed her eyes, but that didn't block out Stuart's angry voice.

'I didn't *touch* my helmet. I told you. I was OK. Someone else must have done it.'

'But —?' The question stuck in Miriam's throat, and Stuart didn't wait for her to finish. He answered it anyway, icy-cold again now.

'It was Hesketh, of course. Who else could it have been? He must have pulled me out because of you.'

'I didn't do a thing,' Miriam said. She wished he would shut up and get on with the game. 'Look, why don't we do this level together? To even things up?'

'Are you *joking?*' Stuart sounded even more furious. 'You've already got ahead of me twice. I'm going to do this one on my own, and find the wheel without you.'

Are you now? Miriam thought. *Well, at least you've told me what we're looking for.* She opened her eyes and saw the room settle down and stop.

Ahead of her, the green door was open wide and she glided straight through, without waiting for Stuart.

Chapter 15

Torn strips of cloth flapped above high, shuttered windows. Miriam stepped into the centre of a small court-yard shadowed by thick stone walls and heard the sound of a gong in the distance. Slowly and warily she turned, staring at the cobbled ground and the little wheels fixed crazily beside the doorways.

On the other side of the courtyard there was a short, thin man. He had a shaved head and he was draped in an orange robe, but Miriam knew that he was Stuart. She could recognize him now by the way he stood, whatever disguise he was wearing. Glancing down at herself, she saw the same bare feet and the same folds of orange cloth.

'Those wheels aren't for us, are they?' she said. 'We're not looking for one like that?'

But Stuart still wasn't speaking to her. He turned away to examine the left-hand side of the courtyard where a small archway led through into another, even smaller yard. The sun slanted dustily across its broken flagstones.

Behind him, on the right, was a pair of massive wooden doors opening into a dark building. The doors were painted with tortured, twisted patterns in red and green and they stood ajar. From behind came the sound of muted, unfamiliar chanting.

Was this place a monastery? Were they monks? Miriam peered round, uneasily. There were too many little, secret windows in the angles of the walls. Too many dark places where people could hide, to watch unobserved. She shuddered.

Stuart glided past her and pushed the big wooden doors open, slipping into the darkness beyond. Miriam pulled a face at his disappearing back. Who said they ought to go that way? Deliberately, she turned her back on the doors, pointing through the arch into the smaller yard.

But she didn't start moving. Instead, there was a flash, and a man in a rough grey tunic leapt into the space under the arch. Above his head he held two curved swords, barring the way through.

'I *want* to go that way!' Miriam said, out loud. She dropped her uselessly pointing hand and took a real step towards him.

Immediately, the swords sliced, criss-cross, chopping the air in front of her. One of the tattered rag banners fluttered between the blades and dropped to the ground in a hundred shreds. The message was clear. *Go this way, and you're dead.*

Was it a test? For a moment, she hesitated. Then the man whirled one of the swords again, almost lazily, and the dusty sunlight flashed bright on the edge of the blade. *Maybe not*, she thought. She would have to follow Stuart after all.

Spinning round, she raised her hand and headed for the doors. As she drew nearer, the sound of chanting increased, and the banners round the doorway fluttered distractingly. She glided between the doors, into the darkness, and found herself in a temple.

. . . *min-now, min-now, min-now* . . .

Closing her mind to the sound, she gazed round the building. It was full of curls of smoke, rising from a thousand tiny lamps, and through the smoke the walls glittered, intricate and mysterious. Twisted gilt pillars snaked up to a roof painted with dim figures and demonic faces, and in every corner and on every ledge there were statues.

They were many-armed or multi-headed, some with smooth skin and yellow, waxy bellies and some with blue, contorted faces. They stood in clusters, rising to the smoky upper reaches of the walls, where shadows swelled and dwindled grotesquely, and the shapes were almost indistinguishable. From every angle they peered down, their glassy eyes catching the light as the lamps flickered.

Miriam stood for a second, wondering how much she was actually seeing and how much her imagination was filling in. Then she raised her voice.

'Stuart? Where are you?'

There was no answer, but something orange fluttered from behind a pillar and she glided towards it, straining her eyes to make out the shapes that crouched in the darkness.

It wasn't Stuart. When she reached the pillar, an orange rag fluttered mockingly over her head and a statue stared down at her from high above.

Bright eyes in the shadows.

A small, uneasy shiver ran down her back, and she screwed up her fists. *Don't be stupid. It's only a game. Only pictures.* But before she could convince herself, there was a slow creak from behind.

She spun round towards the crack of light that showed between the doors. It was shrinking. Slowly, the great doors were swinging shut.

With a crash, they slammed, and the light disappeared completely. The pale, smoky flames of the little oil lamps flickered into tall strands, drawn up by the draught of the slamming.

Then they went out.

Miriam was in thick darkness, blacker than anything she had ever seen in the real, waking world. It lay round her, heavy as felt, and suddenly the Game Helmet seemed like a blindfold, stifling her.

But that was silly! She forced her brain to stay calm. She was perfectly safe in the test room. She wasn't going to bump into anything, as long as she kept still, and the game couldn't go on like this for long. She only had to wait and see what happened. She was perfectly safe . . .

And then the eyes came to life.

Suddenly, on every side, they flickered and began to glow. Yellow and green, brown and icy-pale. Pin-points of

95

light, but each one unmistakably an eye, with white and iris and minute black pupil. Staring through the darkness.

Like the eyes of her nightmare.

But they're not! She struggled to keep her breathing slow, to stay in control. *They haven't got anything to do with the dream. They're just the eyes of those statues. Bits of glass.*

She forced her mind to reconstruct the high walls, with their hundred ledges. The unfamiliar shapes. The contorted bodies, sculptured in stone and wood, moulded from baked clay. Ordinary, straightforward statues.

Swallowing hard, she twisted her head, trying to work out what was making them glitter. They must be reflecting light from somewhere. They must —

And then, away to the right, one pair of eyes flickered. And blinked.

No! She must have made a mistake! It must have been —

Away to the left, still on the edge of her vision, where she couldn't be quite sure of what she was seeing, another pair of eyes moved, and she whisked round, trying to catch the movement before it was over. But the lag of the pictures forced her to close her eyelids and, by the time she looked again, the stare was steady and unwavering.

And then the eyes began to move.

Very slowly, they slid nearer, inching towards her through the darkness. Blinking every now and then. Nearer and nearer. Closer and closer.

'Stuart!'

The word was ripped out of her. She didn't want to call for help. Especially not to him. But she couldn't —

Nearer and nearer came the glassy, staring eyes, swelling towards her. Her heart banged at her ribs, knocking the breath out of her. This couldn't be happening. Not *this*. It was impossible.

Don't look, said her brain. *Screw your eyes up! Hide!*

But that was worse. That was a million times worse. Because if she closed her eyes, they would keep on coming. Only she wouldn't know how close they'd got.

Nearer and nearer . . .

Her pulse raced so hard that she could feel the throb of it in her neck, and under the tight wristband of the Game Glove. And she could hear her breathing, as though it belonged to someone else. Gasping.

She wanted to take the helmet off, to rip open the fastening and get out of the game. But she couldn't, because her whole body was paralysed now. That was part of the dream. The eyes were getting closer and closer, and she couldn't stir. Could hardly breathe.

Locked into the nightmare, she stared helplessly as the eyes came closer and her pulse beat faster and faster. It had to stop soon. It couldn't go on. But it did. Nearer and nearer . . . faster and faster . . .

I can't —

And then, suddenly, the pictures cut out. All the light faded from her helmet, and there was nothing in front of her eyes except the safe, meaningless darkness of the little screens. And Hesketh, standing in the doorway when she pulled the helmet off.

The relief freed her body. She launched herself forward at his huge, immovable bulk, yelling as loud as she could, to make him hear what she was saying.

'There *is* somebody else in the game! Somebody who knows about me! I told you before — there's someone spying on us!'

She crashed straight into him, but he didn't give an inch. He simply caught hold of her shoulders and held her back, at arm's length.

'There's nobody there, Miriam. You're imagining things.'

'But I saw . . . someone knew — '

'It's impossible. This game's protected by all sorts of passwords and barriers. No one can get in.'

Someone can! Someone has! She wanted to scream the words into his face. But he was too solid. Too real and powerful and immovable. With an enormous effort, she steadied her voice and stepped back, out of his hands, forcing herself to talk sense.

'You're wrong. I don't care how impossible it is. I know there's someone watching and interfering. I don't see why you're not worried.'

Hesketh looked down at her. His face was impassive, as heavy as a stone carving. His eyes were dark and unreadable.

'OK,' he said. 'Fine. If you're so sure — prove it to me.'

'That's simple. Whoever this person is, he knows — '

Hesketh shook his head. 'Not like that. I don't want to know what's going on in your head. If this mysterious person knows all about you, he ought to be easy enough to track down. Find out who told him. Then you can get his name — and I can start worrying.'

He smiled. And Miriam saw, suddenly, that it was a challenge. *Go on, then. Think about it seriously.* He was turning her words back at her, to see if she dared to go on.

And she found herself shaking and looking away, like a coward.

Chapter 16

After the sprites had disappeared, Will sat for a long time, staring at the blank screen.

There was something very wrong with the game. It was schizophrenic.

Most of the time it dealt in crude fantasy. Tired stereotypes of foreign countries, with comic enemies, like the Wild West bandits and the killer penguins. It was a straightforward beat-'em-up-and-find-the-treasure game. Except that, in the middle of the clichés, there were sudden touches of — real life.

Like fear.

Will sat and thought about the Intrepid Naturalist, paralysed by the sight of spiders. That had been odd enough. But today's little offering was even odder, because there were no monsters at all. Just — the eyes.

He hadn't even known what they were at first. When the sprites finally got into the temple — after a record amount of squeaking in the octagonal room — he'd looked at all the oil lamps burning away and thought, *OK. This session's about flame-throwing.*

That made it pretty annoying when the screen went pitch-black. He'd peered through the darkness, making out the dim shape of one of the sprites and trying to find the lamps again. Ignoring the tiny dots of light that seemed to be appearing everywhere.

But the lamps were invisible, and there was nothing else to see or hear, except more squeaking, of course. So after a while he decided to see what would happen if he clicked on a dot. Maybe it would change into some kind of light, so that he could see again. Sliding the mouse across the mat, he clicked on the nearest one.

And all the dots blinked at him.

They didn't just blink. They doubled in size as well, and suddenly he saw what they were. Dozens of tiny pairs of eyes, staring out from the darkness.

So? he thought. Eyes didn't seem like a lot of use. Not on their own. Left to himself, he would have stopped there, and never found out what they were for.

But the game gave him a clue. Suddenly, the shadowy little sprite gave a single squeak, so that he looked back at it. And he saw that it was standing absolutely, rigidly still. Just like the Intrepid Naturalist.

Was it the same sprite? Was it scared stiff *again?* That seemed a bit monotonous, but he couldn't ignore the hint. He moved to another eye — because the eyes were the only weapons he had — and clicked on that.

And all the eyes got bigger again.

Click.

And again.

He went on enlarging them, until he began to get the creeps himself. But the sprite didn't move or squeak again. *Boring.* With a last click, he dropped the mouse and sat back to work out what to do next.

And the sprite disappeared.

No fanfare sounded. No score flashed up on the screen. The thing just vanished, without any fuss, and a few seconds later the oil lamps flared up again.

What the — ?

But there was no time to worry about what it all meant, because the other sprite was still there, on the far side of the temple. It was creeping towards the row of prayer wheels at the back.

Oh no, you don't! Will thought. Now he could see again, he knew just what to do. He whisked his arrow over the screen, clicking on everything movable — every statue and oil lamp and prayer flag.

He'd been right about the flame-throwing. Everywhere he clicked, a blazing missile appeared, launching itself

100

straight towards the sprite. He bombarded it as hard as he could, making it dodge and weave.

The screen filled with bursts of fire that blocked the sprite's way, forcing it to change direction and double back, round pillars and into corners. And there was no shortage of new weapons. Every time the picture scrolled, Will saw fresh supplies of statues and flags and lamps.

It was almost too easy. The sequence would have been much better with two sprites to fight. Trying to keep an eye on both of them at once would have been a real challenge. Why had he had to get rid of the other one?

What was the point of that first bit, with the eyes?

The question kept buzzing round in Will's head, interfering with his concentration. Absentmindedly, he began to click on the prayer wheels at the back of the temple — completely forgetting that the sprite had been creeping towards them.

The third wheel didn't change into anything. It flew straight across the screen, just as it was. And the sprite shot out an arm and grabbed it. With a huge flourish, it brandished the wheel high in the air.

Squeak-SQUEAK-squeak!

They weren't real words, but the meaning was as plain as print. Triumph. The sprite had won, and it was gloating, in its own garbled language.

The screen went blank, and Will sat back and chewed at the side of his finger. Slowly, he ran over the whole session in his head, thinking about the fear. And the gloating. And the squeaks.

What did it all mean? It was infuriating that he couldn't save the game. He wanted it there, at his fingertips, so he could run it back and study what had happened, over and over again. But he couldn't work out how to do that. And when he'd asked his father the other night, all he'd got was a shake of the head.

Impossible. The thing's protected like the Crown Jewels.

If his father couldn't do it, then no one could. But . . .

101

Restlessly, Will stood up, prowling through the empty flat, picking up scattered books and clothes and straightening cushions. He had to get a better grip on the game. He had to save something, so that he could go back and look at what happened, without having to concentrate on playing.

He washed up the breakfast things and made himself a sandwich, but the problem teased at his mind. And when he tried to get down to his homework, doodled notes wove themselves into the margin of his maths book. Peculiar things about the game, scrawled illegibly in his small, cramped handwriting.

No proper choice about the levels. Only a mockery of choice, as the sprites squeaked and pointed at the map. Nothing that the player could influence.

No second chances. Whatever was done seemed to be done for ever.

The fear...

The squeaking...

It was the squeaking that bothered him most of all. Why design that into the game? He'd tried a bit of game design himself, and his father always ripped his ideas to shreds. *You've wasted too much memory on unimportant things. Everything in a game uses memory, and memory costs money. So if it's not important or entertaining — leave it out.*

So why wasn't the useless, boring squeaking left out?

It was almost ten o'clock by the time he worked out something he could do. The washing-up was neatly stacked, his homework was done, after a fashion, and he was sitting with his feet up, waiting for his father to come in. As he leant back in the chair, with his head still buzzing, he suddenly saw the big reel-to-reel tape recorder standing in the corner.

Yes!

It was so obvious that he actually laughed out loud, sitting all by himself in the empty flat. He'd been racking his brains to think of a way to save bits of the game, puzzling about programming and video links and cracking security codes, and he'd ignored the most obvious thing of all.

He could record the next lot of squeaking on tape. And see what he could get out of it.

Jumping up, he began to sort through the reels, looking for a tape to use. *Trombone — W, aged 11.* That would do. He hadn't bothered with the trombone since his mother left. He didn't mind recording over that. With his thumbnail, he began to scratch the label off.

And then he stopped.

He wasn't quite sure why. But it had something to do with the unsettling, peculiar nature of the game. He *thought* it was sensible to record the squeaking and try to find out about it. But maybe that was just as dotty as recording space chatter and trying to hear alien voices. Maybe he'd got the wrong idea altogether.

Carefully, he smoothed the label down and slid the reel back on to the shelf. He'd make the recording all right. But he still wouldn't say anything to his father. Not yet.

K & K: ELECTRONIC MEMO
HESKETH BARRINGTON TO JOHN SHELLEY
PRIORITY: NORMAL

The stress test on Subject A was completed successfully this afternoon. As you can see from the monitor charts [attached] the stress monitor worked fine. But I would say, from personal observation of the Subject, that the top stress level may be a bit high.

Should we lower it a bit before the game goes on the market?

K & K: ELECTRONIC MEMO
JOHN SHELLEY TO HESKETH BARRINGTON
PRIORITY: NORMAL

I have consulted about stress levels. A fairly high level of stress is necessary to establish proper attachment to the game. (i.e. if we don't scare the kids enough, they won't get hooked.)

I'll take care of that one. Your job is finishing the tests. AS SOON AS POSSIBLE.

Chapter 17

Miriam knew the nightmare would come that night.

For as long as she could, she lay awake, staring up into the shadows while Rachel snored on the other side of the cabin. Staring — and trying not to think.

But she couldn't keep it up all night. Gradually, the mutters and the creaks, and the lapping of the water faded out of her consciousness. Helplessly, she slid down into the gaping emptiness that waited for her. Into the pit of sleep.

And, instantly, she was there, in the nightmare, with the darkness closing round her, and the panic rising. Inside her head, she heard herself scream.

No!

But her lips didn't move, and there was no sound. Only a thickening of the darkness.

And then the eyes.

One by one, they winked open, glinting from a long way off. Bright and distant as stars in the winter sky. She couldn't scream or look away. She couldn't think them into nonsense. Even in the dream, she could feel her body ache as all the muscles tensed, anticipating the terror.

Then the eyes began to move, centimetre by centimetre, sliding gradually towards her. Almost imperceptibly at first, so that she hoped — as she always hoped — that this time they would be still.

But that was just another part of the dream. A cruel, teasing hope that drained away as the eyes crept nearer. Nearer and nearer, until their lashes spiked the darkness and the network of veins swelled horribly red across the bulging white. Nearer —

And then she woke.

For a moment, she thought she was dead. Everything in her body felt as though it had stopped. Her blood was frozen in her veins, her lungs were paralysed, and she was caught between one heartbeat and the next. *No* . . .

Her mind echoed the shock as she lay rigid, and a voice whispered on and on inside her head. She had never dreamed that voice before, but it seemed to belong, inevitably, to the horror of the nightmare.

. . . *min-now, min-now, min-now* . . .

As soon as she could move, she reached under the bunk for her book and her torch, and pulled the covers shakily over her head. Switching the torch on, she began to read, mouthing the words to make herself concentrate on the story. To shut out everything else.

She wasn't going to risk falling asleep again.

In the morning, Laura took one look at her and pulled a face.

'You look as though you haven't slept a wink all night!'

'I'm fine.' Miriam tried to sound brisk, but it was an effort.

'You're *not*! What on earth —?'

The question was almost there. Laura's mouth was actually shaping the next word, but it never came. Miriam could see her biting it back. Her bright, inquisitive eyes slid away, towards the shopping list.

'Well, you're not going to be much use at the shops,' she said. 'If you come, I'll end up pushing you round in the trolley.'

'Don't be silly. I always help you on Saturdays.'

'So? Have a Saturday off. I'll take the other two, and you can go back to bed and get some more sleep.'

Miriam hesitated. The thought of shopping with Joe and Rachel was horrific, especially this morning. They had to be distracted all the time, so that they didn't annoy Laura. Otherwise she lost her temper dramatically. 'I . . .'

Laura grinned. 'Oh go on, you noddy. It's not the end of the world if I shriek my head off in Sainsbury's. Have a bit of time to yourself. But don't wake your father up. He spent half the night going through the wretched bank statement and he'll drop to bits if he doesn't sleep in.' Laura rolled her eyes up at the ceiling. 'You two! You haven't got an ounce of red blood between you. I ought to feed you on tintacks.'

Miriam grinned weakly, and Laura pointed to the back of the boat.

'*Sleep!*'

'OK. Fine,' Miriam said. 'Thanks.' And she lurched back into the cabin and fell on her bunk.

But sleep was the last thing she wanted. She kept her nightdress on, but as soon as she heard the car crunch away across the gravel she got up and pulled on a jumper. Making herself a big mug of strong coffee, she went outside and climbed on to the cabin roof.

It was very peaceful sitting there, looking up and down the towpath. There was a scatter of half a dozen houseboats along the bank, but all the others had their curtains firmly drawn, and she was alone in the pale, mild sunshine.

She let her eyes wander over the familiar river bank. The worn path and the rubbish bins. The froth of old man's beard cascading over the bushes and the delicate, shifting play of light on the surface of the water. Reality.

She tried to tell herself that it was beautiful. The only thing that counted. But the bright, dangerous scenes of the New World scrawled themselves across her mind, mocking the pale water and the old man's beard. After a moment, she tucked her knees up under her nightdress, took a sip of coffee and shut her eyes.

She had been sitting there for ten or fifteen minutes when she heard the sound of feet coming down the path. Not a jogger. Someone walking rather slowly. With her eyes still closed, she turned away, towards the middle of the river, and waited for the feet to pass.

But they drew level with her and stopped, and a voice said, rather hesitantly, 'Hallo?'

107

For an instant, sitting peacefully on the roof, Miriam was tempted to pretend she hadn't heard. To keep her eyelids closed and wait for the feet to go away.

But there was something — unexpected — about the voice. Slowly, she turned towards the bank and opened her eyes.

To see a stranger. A tall, gangling boy with glasses. Fifteen, maybe, or even sixteen. He was staring straight at her and she was suddenly, acutely, aware that she was still in her nightdress. She felt her face turn pink.

He was looking embarrassed too, but he took a step nearer. 'Miriam?'

And then she realized. 'You're *Stuart*!'

He grinned, nervously. 'It's peculiar, isn't it? I've been imagining you all wrong. When I saw you in the teleconference, I thought you were fat. But you aren't at all.'

'And I thought you were — short.' Miriam pulled her nightdress down hard over her knees. 'How did you find me?'

'The boat. I mean, I knew you lived on a boat. And you had to be close enough to get to K & K after school. So I worked out where the river was near enough, and then I went to the library. To look up your parents on the electoral register.'

'David and Laura Enderby.' Miriam nodded. 'It sounds very complicated.'

'Oh no!' Stuart said, earnestly. 'It only took me an hour and a half. I did it last night, after we'd finished playing.'

'Why bother?'

His smile disappeared, and suddenly she recognized him properly. He *was* the person she'd seen on the screen when they were teleconferencing. The boy who tried too hard and came too close. He was just six inches taller than she'd expected, that was all.

'I think we ought to talk,' he said.

'What do you want to talk about?'

'The game, of course.' He flushed suddenly. 'We've *got* to talk about it, haven't we?'

'But we're not allowed to. Remember? *You don't try to contact each other outside the game.*'

Stuart snorted. And that was familiar too. 'Those rules aren't laws. The worst they can do if we break them is chuck us out of the tests. And this is—this might be important enough for that.'

Miriam sat and stared at him for a moment more. Then she slid off the roof and waved at the boat. 'You'd better come in. Before the hordes get back from shopping.'

She made him some coffee, and they sat facing each other, awkwardly cradling the mugs in their hands. Now they were inside, Stuart seemed even less confident. He sat hunched forward on the bench, sipping coffee and gazing down at his shoes.

'Well?' Miriam said impatiently.

'I . . .' He hesitated, and then the words came out in a rush. 'What happened to you yesterday? After I went into the temple?'

Miriam's mouth tightened. 'I could ask the same question. When I got inside, you'd vanished.'

'No . . . I didn't mean—' She'd confused him, and he turned his mug miserably round and round in his hands. 'I meant . . . well, I heard you shout.'

Miriam looked him straight in the eye. 'I was startled,' she lied. 'That was all. As soon as I got into the place, the lights went out.'

'But when they came on again—you weren't there.'

'So?' She said it lightly, fending him off. She might have made a fool of herself, but there was no reason why she should spill it all out to him.

And then she looked down and saw his hands.

They were shaking. Shaking so hard that his coffee slopped from side to side. And the fingers round the mug were clenched tight, almost hiding the pattern.

He saw her looking. Putting the mug down, he pushed his hands into his pockets. 'That's all right then. I mean — if you're OK. I just came to see if you were . . . well, if you *were* OK. And you are, so — '

He scrambled to his feet and headed for the door, looking awkward and wretched. Miriam leaned back on her bench, watching him go. Feeling light with relief.

But he stopped at the bottom of the companionway. For a long moment, he looked down at her, still trembling on the verge of going.

Then he said, abruptly, 'I thought it might be like me and the spiders.'

'The . . . spiders?'

'That's right.' The effort of speaking made him sound fierce. 'That's what I came to talk about. It's silly to go away without saying it.'

Miriam sat very still. 'So?' she said softly.

Stuart swallowed. 'I — they're my thing. Spiders. They really scare me.'

'But you said — '

He went red again. 'Of course I did. You try being a boy and telling something like that to a girl you don't even know properly. *Yeah, I was scared sick. Little Miss Muffet in person. Show me anything with eight legs and I'm a jelly.*'

His voice was loud and harsh. And miserable. Miriam could hear the anger, and the way he loathed himself for being afraid, and she knew what he was offering. He was giving her a chance to tell the truth about the game. All she had to do was respond — tell him about the eyes — and she wouldn't be alone any more.

All.

Clenching her hands tight, she tried to put the words together inside her head. *It was like that for me . . . You're not the only one who's scared . . .*

But she hesitated too long. While she was still trying to find the courage to speak, Stuart took three steps towards her. Coming too close.

'Don't you *see*?' he hissed. 'If we've *both* been scared like that, it means the game's fixed. It's homed straight in on our private nightmares.'

Miriam looked up at him, and he came even closer. Behind the thick glasses, his eyes were blazing.

'Think of all the other frightening things that could have happened. Snakes and heights. Monsters and knives. Being laughed at and chased and shut up in boxes. There are millions of scary things. But we've met the ones that scare us most, and that means — '

He took a deep breath and leaned down, so that his face was only a hand's breadth from Miriam's. She could feel him trembling.

' — it means that *someone's told them about us.*'

It was like having her head ripped open. He'd smashed through her defences, aiming straight for the thing she'd been fighting to ignore and avoid. Before she knew what she was doing, Miriam was on her feet, yelling at him. Shouting into his face at point blank range.

'Get out of here! You're insane! Get *out*!'

His mouth opened, and she saw him struggle for words, but they never came. Instead, he turned and stumbled up the steps, banging his head on the door frame as he raced out of the boat. Miriam heard him running away down the towpath and she drew a long, deep breath. Leaning over the table, she rested her weight on her hands and closed her eyes.

When her heart stopped thudding, she opened her eyes slowly and saw her father standing in the doorway of the back cabin, in his pyjamas. He was staring at her.

'I — ' But she couldn't speak.

He didn't move towards her. 'Do you want to tell me about it?' he said.

'I — ' For a second, she longed for him to insist. To *make* her tell, so that she could ask the question that she didn't dare spell out, even to herself.

111

But he would never do that. He would listen to anything she wanted to say, but she had to start things off. To speak the first, unforgivable words. If she could . . .

He took a step into the cabin. 'Minnow?'

And, immediately, she knew she couldn't do it. Shaking her head, she backed away. 'I — it really doesn't matter, Dad. I'm sorry I woke you up. It was just a silly quarrel.'

She turned and escaped into her own cabin, closing the door behind her. Crawling back into bed, she pulled the covers over her head.

But it was too late for that. The question had been asked now. Who was interfering with the game? Who was using her nightmare and Stuart's fear of spiders?

And how did he know?

Lying there under the covers, she knew she would have to talk to Stuart after all. However much he irritated her, he was the only person who would understand. The only person she *could* talk to about the game.

But how could she get in touch with him now?

Chapter 18

It had been simple enough for Stuart to find her. She was called Enderby, and her home was on a boat. But how on earth could she find Stuart *Jones*, who lived in a house? There were six columns of Joneses in the telephone directory. She couldn't check them all.

The only thing she knew about him, outside the game, was that his father worked for K & K. That was no help at all. She could hardly ask Hesketh which department he was in — not unless she wanted him to know she was breaking the rules. She might just as well chase Christine Riley's car through the streets.

Wryly, Miriam imagined herself in a jogging suit, haring after the green estate car. A pity she had to go to K & K. Following Christine to Stuart's would have solved all her problems about tracking him down.

As it was, there didn't seem to be any solution. She brooded about it all the weekend, but she couldn't see any way of tracking Stuart down.

And then, as she walked out of school on Monday afternoon, everything suddenly fell into place. As she reached the gate, she glanced right and saw Christine Riley, caught behind the traffic lights.

At that precise moment, a bicycle bell sounded from behind. Jumping out of the way, Miriam looked round to see Connie swooping towards her. With the same steady smile that had been on her face in the Drama cupboard.

'Hey!' Miriam said, almost without thinking. Connie slowed down and scooted along beside her, pushing at the ground with one leg.

'Mmm?'

'You know . . .' If there'd been time to think, Miriam could never have asked. The words would have clogged

113

her throat. But the lights were already changing and, if she hesitated, the chance would be lost for ever. 'You know you said you'd help? Without any questions.'

Connie's eyes widened, but she didn't say anything. She just nodded.

'Look at the traffic lights,' Miriam muttered. 'See that green estate car?'

Connie nodded again, watching it.

'Well . . .' Miriam swallowed. '. . . do you think you could follow it? Find out where it goes?'

For a second, Connie's eyebrows went up, and she stared. It was the only time that Miriam had ever seen her taken completely off guard.

But it was only for a second. Then, as the cars surged forward, she was on her bike, swinging out through the gate.

'Phone me when you get home,' she called over her shoulder, and she was gone, her long legs pumping the pedals and her bag bumping crazily on her back.

And Miriam turned away, towards the bus stop. And remembered who it was that she was going to see.

She spent the bus journey in a panic, with her hands clenched tightly in her lap. It was impossible to believe that Hesketh wouldn't guess what she'd just done. Somehow — from a tell-tale flicker of her eyes, or simply by magic — he would see that she had broken the rules and talked to Stuart. That she was trying to find him again, even while she was walking into the game.

He would know.

But he didn't. He gave her one sharp look as she walked into the building.

'OK?'

'I'm fine,' she said stiffly.

And that was it. Hustling her down to the test room, he let her in and walked off straight away, leaving her to get started on her own. Miriam drew a long, deep breath.

114

It was all right so far. Now she mustn't give herself away while she was playing. She would have to be very careful how she talked to Stuart in the game.

But when she put on her helmet, she found that she couldn't talk to him at all. The rainbow room was already spinning, but there was no sign of anyone in it.

That didn't make sense. She stared round, looking for Stuart, but he wasn't there. Frowning, she closed her eyes.

It was a silence that made her open them again.

Until that moment, there had always been some kind of noise in the game. A faint rattle from the spinning doors. The rustle of leaves in the jungle. The wind over the snow, and the distant chanting in the temple. Sound had been part of the background, helping to change the atmosphere from one continent to another.

But this silence was complete.

Turning her head, she saw that the yellow door had swung open. Which continent—? But the question died in her mind before she had spelt it out, and the stillness beyond the door took possession of her.

She was staring at a wide, flat scrubland, stained reddish-brown by the dying light of the sun. Rusty earth showed bare between scattered clumps of grass and stunted bushes. Beyond, a huge rock reared up, massive and flat-topped. As the sunset caught it, it glowed an extraordinary, vibrant red.

For a moment, Miriam was almost afraid to move. Then, very slowly, she raised her hand.

She meant to look down at herself as she passed through the door, to try and guess where she was by seeing how she changed. But, as she crossed the threshold, a huge shape bounded straight at her.

Boi-oi-oi-oing!

The brown body was so close that, for a moment, it was actually too big to recognize. And before she had recovered, another one bounced at her. And another.

Boi-oi-oi-oing! Boi-oi-oi-oing!

115

She was in the middle of a crowd of comic, cartoon kangaroos. They bounded all round, staring with big eyes and fluttering ridiculous eyelashes. And every time they jumped, there was a loud twanging noise, as laughable as the kangaroos themselves.

Boi-oi-oi-oing!

It was a shocking contrast to the stillness of the huge red rock and the spreading plain. Miriam blinked and looked round.

'Hey! Stuart!'

There was no answer. Maybe he was hidden behind one of the bushes. She turned towards the biggest one and raised her hand.

Boi-oi-oi-oing!

The ground seemed to jerk from under her feet. Then it came smacking back towards her. Looking down, she saw her long pale feet hit the ground and push off again, sending her shooting into the air a second time.

She was a kangaroo!

Turning back to the rest of the bouncing crowd, she waved her arms frantically, and yelled again. 'Stuart! This is me! Where are you?'

One of the kangaroos came out of the crowd, towards her. It didn't make a sound, but it lifted its silly little arm and pointed at the rock on the horizon.

Why didn't he speak? Miriam raised her voice. 'You think we ought to go there?'

There was still no answer. Instead, the other kangaroo began to bound away towards the rock. What was he doing? Sulking? Miriam squared her shoulders. Well, he wasn't going to get ahead of her. She set off after him, struggling to get used to the leaping.

It was a weird sensation. All her muscles said that she was standing still, but her eyes told her that she was bounding across an enormous plain, with jumps that took her a metre or more up into the air. And she couldn't close her

116

eyes, because she had to keep track of the shape ahead of her, as it zigzagged across the scrubland.

They had almost reached the rock when the kangaroo stopped suddenly, pointing down at the ground.

'What are we doing?' Miriam called. 'Why have you stopped?'

No answer. Gritting her teeth, she bounded on, until she caught up and saw what was blocking their way.

A deep, narrow chasm split the ground in front of them. It was no more than three metres wide, but it stretched from side to side of the landscape, as far as Miriam could see. There was no way to reach the red rock without crossing it.

She frowned. 'Can we jump over?'

The other kangaroo stood very still, staring at her. Then, without any warning, it bounced. First it moved to the left, punching at empty air, and then it jumped straight at Miriam, jabbing her in the chest.

And the world went head over heels.

It was crazy. The scrub swooped towards her face and the red rock went flying up over the back of her head. For an instant, everything seemed to move in slow motion. Wrenching her head towards the other kangaroo, Miriam opened her mouth to scream at it. *Why did you do that? What's going on?*

Then she realized that he was higher than she was. And as she tilted her head back to look up at the great kangaroo-face, a white balloon swelled out of its mouth. A speech bubble.

Ha! Ha! Ha!

Then the balloon popped, and everything was whizzing past her at normal speed. And she understood that she was falling. Even though she still felt upright, her game body was tumbling through the air, falling down into the deep, dark chasm.

Stuart had pushed her over the edge.

She grabbed at the rim of the ground, but it crumbled in her hands and she plunged into the semi-darkness, head first. There was just enough light to see the rocky sides of the chasm sliding past, at sickening speed.

Up, said her sense of gravity.

Down, said her eyes and her brain.

Up . . . down . . . up . . . down . . . She was still trying to get it straight when she hit the bottom with a loud, ringing thud. And dozens of brilliant stars burst round her in the gloom.

Not again! she thought, furiously. *I'm dead again!*

But the stars dissolved and she was still there, at the bottom of the crack, gazing up towards the narrow line of blue sky and the kangaroo-face, high above her.

She was so angry that she almost choked.

Stuart had done it to her. *Stuart!* That mild, eager idiot. She'd shouted at him on Saturday, so he'd pushed her out of the game and sent her tumbling down into the darkness. Why had she ever thought she could *talk* to him?

Flinging her head back, she yelled at the top of her voice, spitting the words up at the smug, staring face.

'You're *despicable*, Stuart Jones! A pathetic, hateful, unfeeling toad! If I ever get hold of you . . . '

She didn't wait to reach home before she phoned Connie. The moment she got off the bus, she ran to the nearest phone box. Her fingers were shaking so much that she dropped her coin three times before she managed to push it into the slot.

'Connie? Did you manage it? Did you keep up?'

And Connie's voice came back, blissfully calm.

'She went to thirty-six Beauchamp Terrace. The one with the roses in the front garden.'

Chapter 19

Both the sprites were still squeaking when the game cut out and the screen went blank. Will leaned forward and clicked off all the switches. Computer, monitor, tape recorder. Then he leaned back in his chair and let out his breath.

For a while, at the start of the session, his plan had looked like a failure. Now he *wanted* the sprites to squeak, they seemed to have lost their voices. When they were in the octagonal room, neither of them had made a sound. They'd moved round independently, each one ignoring the other, as if it were invisible.

Then they'd gone through the door and changed into a herd of kangaroos.

Will grinned. That had almost done for him. He hadn't known which kangaroos to concentrate on, and he'd wasted ages trying to move bushes and stir up the dusty earth. He'd nearly given up when — as a last resort — he clicked on one of the kangaroos and found that he could control it.

After that, it was easy. He spotted the chasm, half-way across the screen, and picked out the two kangaroos who weren't bouncing. They had to be his enemies. The two grey sprites, in disguise. Now if only they would follow him . . .

It worked like a charm. They followed him across the bare, red ground and as soon as they reached the chasm —

Boi-oi-oi-oing — POW!

Boi-oi-oi-oing — POW!

He toppled them over like skittles and they went tumbling down into the darkness, side by side.

That should get you squeaking! Will thought triumphantly. The sprites always made more noise when things weren't moving. Now they were trapped down a hole, he expected them to put their heads together and have a real kangaroo committee.

They didn't. They went on ignoring each other, exactly the same as before, but they didn't disappoint him. Throwing their heads back, they began to squeak at full blast, sometimes one after the other and sometimes both together. And they didn't stop until the end of the game, when everything vanished.

It was brilliant. He must have recorded three or four minutes of solid squeaking. If he couldn't get anything out of that, there was nothing there.

He wanted to get going straight away. To start running the tape backwards and forwards, at different speeds, hunting for some kind of message. But he knew he would miss things unless he had a proper system, so he sat still for a moment and worked it out.

He'd check the instructions for the tape recorder and list all the tricks it could play. Then he'd work out every possible combination of tricks and try them all methodically, keeping a proper record.

Sliding out of his chair, he went across the lobby, to the door opposite. His father's room was more like an office than anything else, with a bed jammed into the corner by the desk. A mad inventor's room. Grinning, Will stepped over stacks of books and papers and pulled out the bottom drawer of the filing cabinet.

Most of his father's stuff was stored on disk, but the filing cabinet was still crammed. There were files bulging with letters and sketches, files full of strange doodles and half-finished calculations — and the file that held all the instruction booklets.

Will found it and pulled at the top, but it was jammed in too tight. As he tugged, the file in front erupted, spilling its contents everywhere, and dozens of newspaper cuttings tumbled on to the floor.

He scooped them up and tried to push them straight back into the file, but the other files had expanded to fill the space. The only thing to do was pull everything out and start again.

Taking the cuttings file out, he opened it on the floor and grinned again as he read the top headline.

A NIGHTMARE IN YOUR GARAGE?

Whatever was that doing there? He leaned over, reading the rest of it.

> Virtual Reality is the Next Big Thing in the game world. Major games companies are scrambling to develop 'garage VR' that would operate in any medium-sized space — like an ordinary garage — and cost just a few hundred pounds.
>
> Instead of zapping aliens on screen, children could soon be donning Game Helmets — AND MEETING THEM FACE TO FACE!

Oh, big deal. Trust the papers to make news out of something that had been around for years. Ever since he could remember, all the big companies had been 'on the verge of bringing out home VR'.

Then the paragraph below caught his eye.

> But now experts are questioning the whole idea, because 'real' aliens could be dangerously frightening. They could even cause 'game trauma' — acute and damaging fear that leaves a child psychologically crippled. And the games companies could land up paying millions of pounds in damages.
>
> Unless they find a way to control fear itself.

Slowly, Will flipped up the cutting, to read the memo that was stapled to the back of it. It was addressed to his father, and it was short and to the point.

How's this for dirty tricks? I thought you needed to see the actual cutting, so you knew the worst. This scare could cost us millions, if we don't zap it before we bring the game out.

Time for a few experiments with fear, I think. You've got six weeks. Good luck, buddy!

Will didn't know what it meant. But his fingers shook as he folded it up and he didn't put it back. Instead, he slipped it into his pocket and replaced the cuttings file in the drawer.

Then he found the tape recorder instructions and walked back to his bedroom, reading them as he went.

Chapter 20

Got him! Miriam put the phone down and stepped out of the telephone box, closing the door gently behind her. Then she leaned back against it and took a long breath, forcing herself to keep still and think sensibly.

Not yet.

The black anger was still pounding in her head, drumming up pictures of her flying through the dark streets to Beauchamp Terrace. She could almost feel the thud of her fists, banging against the door, and the hoarse, yelling frenzy of her voice. *Cheat! Liar! You tried to soften me up, didn't you? You wanted to find out my weak spot, so you could win. But I'm not weak! I'm strong, strong, STRONG! And I'm going to make you sorry —*

No sense in that. She would only be making a fool of herself. It was dark and late. By the time she found out where Beauchamp Terrace was, it would be even later, and Stuart would be surrounded by his whole family. What she wanted was to get him on his own, and make him squirm.

Tomorrow.

She turned down towards the river, walking quietly, trying to cage her anger until she needed it. But she hadn't allowed for the way her blood was racing. She had come straight out of the game, blazing with rage, and her whole body was impatient for action. It was agony to keep calm and smile as she stepped on to the boat. Torture to fiddle around answering Rachel and Joe's silly questions, and taking them *very last* drinks of water, after they'd been put to bed.

She wanted . . . she wanted . . .

Her pen trailed over the paper as she dawdled through her homework, sitting in the main cabin. And when Laura got up to make the coffee, she suddenly heard herself say, 'Dad?'

'Mmm?' He looked at her over the top of a pile of bills.

No! I don't want— But she was launched now. Her voice was asking the question.

'Did you ever . . . have anything to do with computers?'

Her father smiled, as though she'd said something amusing. 'Computers? Me?'

'Oh, not *using* them. I didn't mean that. But have you ever had . . . friends, for example? Who worked for computer firms.'

He pushed the bills away, but before he could get a word out, Laura came erupting through the kitchen door, waving a coffee cup in one hand.

'Don't *remind* me! When I met him, he didn't have any *other* friends. Every party we went to was solid computer boredom. It's a wonder Rachel wasn't born with a digital brain!'

Miriam's father smiled. 'They weren't that bad. Just a bit obsessive.'

'Don't give me that,' Laura said. 'They were dire! They used to come round every night—to *your* house—and sit there talking about bits and bytes and ROM and RAM. Ignoring you completely. I used to get so mad—'

'They were fine when we were playing cricket.'

'No, they weren't! They treated you like a moron.' Laura whisked round, appealing to Miriam. 'Look at it like this. I'd just fallen in love with this beautiful man—this *angel*—and I had to watch a crowd of computer louts putting him down. And I couldn't get him to stand up for himself. He just sat there in a corner, letting them waste his time. Letting them sneer at him while they drank his beer. Wouldn't *you* have been furious?'

'I—' Miriam could imagine it, horribly clearly. The jolly, laughing men with their heads together and beer glasses in their hands. And, in the corner, her father, smiling his gentle, self-effacing smile. Laughing at their jokes and not complaining when they shut him out of the conversation.

She looked away from him, furious at Laura for conjuring up the picture. For making her see it.

'I don't think they sneered,' her father said, mildly.

'They didn't get the chance after we were married,' Laura said stoutly. 'I said I wasn't going to have them in the house — and I meant it.'

Watching her standing there, waving the coffee cup with her eyes blazing, Miriam could imagine that too. Laura leaping into battle to defend the man she'd married. Glowing with good intentions and unselfish rage. That was what she was always like. Fierce and impetuous and heroic. As if she were trying to make up for the weaknesses of . . . other people.

And the person she was defending?

Miriam sneaked an embarrassed, sideways look at her father. His expression took her by surprise. He was smiling at Laura, and his face was tender and amused and affectionate. As if —

As if he were the one protecting Laura.

All the patterns in Miriam's mind jumbled together, like beads in a kaleidoscope. Before she could retrieve them, the kettle shrieked in the kitchen, and Laura dived back through the door, to make the coffee. Miriam made a last, awkward grab at finding out what she wanted to know.

'Did I ever meet any of those people? Did they . . . know about me?'

Her father shrugged. Miriam thought he was going to say something, but he didn't get the chance, because Laura stuck her head through the kitchen door again.

'That's a peculiar question. Why do you want to know? You're not telling me you've met one of the rotten old bores? At these K & K tests?'

'I'm not telling *you* anything!' Miriam snapped. 'I wasn't talking to you!'

The words exploded before she could stop herself. Out of the corner of her eye, she saw her father flinch and, for a moment, the whole scene was like a diagram of their

125

life—Laura's question, her own shrinking away from it, and her father's useless, ineffectual regret. That was *their* pattern, and they were frozen into it. She wished . . .

But what could she do? Give in? Give her whole life over to Laura, to be prodded and poked around?

'We were having a private conversation,' she said stiffly.

But her father was turning back to his bills. It was a signal and, for the first time, Miriam understood what he meant when he drew back like that. He was refusing to shut Laura out. If something was a secret from her, he didn't want to know about it. It was part of the protection.

What about me? Miriam wanted to yell. *Don't I need protecting too?*

But that meant giving herself away and letting them in. It would be as bad—as *feeble*—as racing round to Stuart's and hammering on the door in the dark. She couldn't do it.

Instead, she slid across the cabin and picked up the street map, flicking through the index to find Beauchamp Terrace. It took her a long time to pinpoint it, because she was distracted by the sound of her father's pen, scribbling away behind her. She knew he was trying to make things fit, to stretch what he earned so that it would pay all the bills.

He would have earned more working with computers . . .

Putting her hands over her ears, Miriam frowned at the web of lines on the map, struggling to concentrate on the street names. Forcing herself to read every tiny word. So that her mind wouldn't stray to those jolly, laughing men with their glasses of beer.

. . . *min-na, min-na, min-na* . . .

The next day, she set off for Beauchamp Terrace, as soon as she came out of school. Connie was with her, and she raised an eyebrow as Miriam turned left.

'Want me to come?'

So far, she had kept her promise. She hadn't asked anything about the green car, or about the house where it had led her. But Miriam could feel the effort she was making to hold the questions back. They were all there, below the surface, waiting to break out the moment there was a chance.

'No thanks. I'll go on my own.'

Connie looked at her carefully for a moment. Then she nodded and set off home without another word. Miriam headed for a different bus stop, to catch a bus she'd never used before.

As it pulled away from the kerb, she saw Debbie dawdling out of school, chatting to Stella. Suddenly, she realized how long it was since they had walked home together, giggling and gossiping. It seemed like a different life. Now she was shut in with fears and puzzles that she couldn't share with anyone, and that kind of chatter seemed like a million miles away.

Another world.

She pressed her face to the glass, watching for Beauchamp Terrace. It was almost half-past four by the time she got off the bus and began to walk along, looking at the numbers. She saw the roses when she was still fifty yards away, big shrubs with blackening leaves and a few late flowers. They had dropped most of their petals on to the pavement and she skirted them delicately as she opened the front gate.

She meant to march straight up to the front door. To ring the bell boldly, and ask for Stuart. But when she was only half-way down the path, she saw that it wasn't that simple, because there were three different bells. The house was divided into flats, and the names on the labels were blurred and hard to read.

The sensible thing would have been to ring one at random, and ask where Stuart lived. But she was nervous, and she didn't like the idea that he might overhear her asking. Why should he have a warning, a chance to get ready to meet her? She wanted to spring on him, out of nowhere.

Instead of going right up to the front door, she turned left and slipped through the side gate and along the wall of the house, into the back garden. It was tangled and secret, full of big shaggy evergreens and thick creepers, and Miriam caught herself looking left and right, watching for enemies.

The whole thing reminded her of the game, as though the real world were coming properly alive at last. She was keyed up—in battle alert—but she didn't really believe that anything would hurt her. Whatever was inside the house was just another problem that she had to crack.

She wouldn't know what she was looking for until she saw it and, to begin with, all she could see was empty rooms. There was no one in the bedroom on the ground floor, nor in the kitchen. She couldn't see into any of the upstairs part of the house, and when she tried the kitchen door, very gently, it was locked. Maybe there was no one in at all.

She was on the verge of going away, and abandoning the whole thing, when a movement caught her eye, and she realized that there was a basement room, opening on to a narrow sunken area, its window almost level with her feet. Crouching behind a bush, she peered in.

Over on the far side of the room, someone was sitting. A tall boy, with dark hair. Miriam caught her breath. He was there. If she made a noise, he would hear her, but as long as she kept calm she could watch him and choose when to show herself.

Kneeling on the bare earth, she went on staring. The room was crammed with expensive equipment and glossy magazines and there were books stacked beside the bed and a table tennis table propped against the wall. Over on the far side, where the boy was working, she could see a computer. And a big reel-to-reel tape recorder.

The boy kept turning from one to the other, pressing keys and fiddling with knobs, but he never turned far enough for Miriam to see his face. She leaned round the bush, trying to catch a glimpse of it, moving silently, because the window between them was very slightly open.

Suddenly, there was an enormous yell from one of the loudspeakers hung on the wall. It boomed through the window at full volume, and Miriam forgot all about keeping hidden. She jerked to her feet, staring into the room with her mouth wide open. Gazing at the loudspeaker as the sound came pouring out.

You're despicable, Stuart Jones! A pathetic, hateful, unfeeling toad! If I ever get hold of you . . .

It *couldn't* be her own voice!

Unsteadily, she clutched at the bush that was shielding her. She knocked its branches against the window and they squeaked over the glass — just as the voice coming over the loudspeaker paused for a second.

Immediately, the boy spun round. Miriam lifted her head defiantly, so that he would see that she was the one in charge. She *wasn't* going to apologize.

But the defiance lasted only a split second. Because the boy wasn't Stuart at all. He was the same height, but he looked quite different, with a flat, freckled face.

For one, dreadful instant, the two of them stared at each other, struck dumb and motionless. And the tape went on running.

. . . you're a sneaking, devious cheat . . .

Then Miriam whisked round and, like lightning, the boy did the same, heading for the door of his room. Panicking, Miriam looked down the garden, but there was no escape there. It was enclosed by a high brick wall, and the only way out was the alley down the side of the house.

Desperately she raced towards it. The strange boy had already vanished, and she expected him to come bursting through the kitchen door at any moment. Feet slithering on the side path, she ran as fast as she could, straining her ears for the sound of an opening door behind her. But it didn't come.

And, too late, she realized why. She'd been expecting the wrong thing. As she flung herself into the front garden, a hand snaked round the corner and grabbed her. The boy had been waiting there, knowing that she had to come through the gate.

But Miriam had the advantage of speed. And fear. 'Let go!' she yelled. 'I haven't done anything. Let *go!*' Twisting sideways, she wrenched at her arm.

The boy was taller and more solid than she was, and she didn't really expect to break free. But as she spoke, his mouth fell open. He was utterly startled. Knocked right off balance.

Seizing the chance, Miriam dragged herself out of his hands and leapt down the path and on to the pavement. Even then she was lucky to get away. He tore after her, but he skidded on the rose petals and crashed to the ground. By the time he'd scrambled to his feet again, she was round the corner and away.

Chapter 21

Will stood staring after her, and her voice hammered in his ears.

Let go! I haven't done anything. Let go!

It couldn't be true. He must have been confused after all those hours of listening to the tape. How could a person speak with *that* voice? It was an electronic illusion. A piece of computer-generated wizardry.

And yet . . .

Slowly, he turned back indoors, walking downstairs and into the flat. He was trying to remember the strange girl's voice. Fixing it in his head, so that he didn't get muddled up. When he was sure he had it, he went over to the tape recorder and rewound the tape he had made.

He'd been over the moon when he heard the shout just now. Full of triumph at having unscrambled the tape and produced a recognizable voice, speaking real words. But he hadn't paid much attention to the words themselves, or to what kind of voice he was hearing. This time, he switched on and listened very carefully. And the yell from the game rang out, exactly the same as before.

You're despicable, Stuart Jones! A pathetic, hateful, unfeeling toad! If I ever get hold of you, I'll make you sorry you ever heard of these tests . . .

He stopped the tape, and swallowed. There was no doubt about it. No possible doubt. It was deep for a girl's voice, with a faint hint of huskiness, but it was hers all right. The voice of the girl who'd shouted at him.

The spy.

But what had she been spying on? And who was it she'd expected to see? Not him, for sure. She'd been shocked rigid when he turned round and she saw his face.

And yet, somehow or other, she was linked to the game he was playing. The sprites were only patterns of light on a computer screen, but one of them spoke with her voice. And what did it say?

You're despicable, Stuart Jones . . .

Stuart Jones. Will closed his eyes. That was a very common name. Just because it had turned up on the tape, it didn't necessarily mean . . . it *couldn't* mean . . .

He ran the tape on a bit further, until the girl's voice stopped for breath, and the other sprite's voice started up. Leaning forward, with his elbows on the desk and his chin in his hands, he heard the furious, bitter screeching.

You think you're so clever, don't you? Too clever to be scared! I trusted you, and you've spat it straight back in my face.

It was loud and fierce — almost confident. But he knew the sound all right. He'd heard it often enough. For a long time, he sat without moving, looking at the blank computer screen. Trying to work out what it meant that Jojo Jones had something to do with this game. Trying to drown out the words of the newspaper cutting that echoed in his head.

. . . children could soon be donning Game Helmets . . . dangerously frightening . . .

That couldn't have any link with this game. He didn't know what Christine did when she hacked in to get him set up — *too complicated for you,* his father said — but no casual hacker could get into a VR session. It would have to be set up from inside, by someone who knew about VR.

Someone who'd been working on it for years, maybe.

Will didn't turn the tape recorder on again. He took out the tape and slid it away into the box that said *Trombone — W, aged 11.* When his father came home, he was out in the kitchen, with his sleeves rolled up, chopping onions to make a nut loaf. He didn't turn round, or say anything. He just nodded, without looking up, and kept his eyes on the sharp edge of the knife as it chopped down, over and over again.

K & K: ELECTRONIC MEMO
JOHN SHELLEY TO HESKETH BARRINGTON
PRIORITY: URGENT

I'm being leaned on very hard. Promotions have
picked up rumours about competition from Sega and
they're desperate to go ahead. Can I give them the
OK?

The rest of the tests are just a formality, aren't they?

K & K: ELECTRONIC MEMO
HESKETH BARRINGTON TO JOHN SHELLEY
PRIORITY: URGENT

I HAVE GOT TO HAVE TWO MORE SESSIONS —
otherwise I'll jack the whole thing in. Tell Promotions
to hold off until I give the OK.

Chapter 22

'So you think this boy's been interfering?' Connie said. 'Hacking into your game?' It was the very first question.

When Miriam appeared on the doorstep, breathless and desperate, she had taken her in without a word. And she'd listened while Miriam poured out everything about Hesketh and the game and what had happened. Now she leaned back against her bedroom wall and looked over the top of her coffee cup.

'It all sounds pretty far-fetched to me.'

'But it *fits*.' Miriam frowned. 'I knew there was someone messing around, right from the beginning. Because my gun got snatched, in the Wild West. And when that flaming torch came at me in Antarctica — someone *guessed* which way I was going to move. If this boy's got my voice on tape, he must be in on it. There has to be a connection.'

Connie shrugged. 'What about that woman in the green car? I saw her go to his house.'

'Christine?' Miriam thought of Christine Riley's sensible, cheerful face and tried to imagine it. 'You think she's up to something? Working for someone else?'

'I don't see why not.' Connie stretched out her long legs and took a sip of coffee. 'Sounds like the obvious explanation.'

'That she's trying to wreck the tests? But how could she — ' Miriam stopped.

'How could she know your secrets?' Connie said. She looked thoughtfully at Miriam for a moment. Then she leaned forward and put down her cup. 'Look — I know you don't like people snooping, but we're just fooling around, aren't we? Why don't you tell me what's really bugging you?'

Miriam stared down at her hands. 'Why does anything have to be bugging me? I just want to know what's going on.'

'That's not what you said in the Drama cupboard. You weren't playing the great detective then. You sounded more like the victim.'

'I . . .'

Slowly, Miriam ran a finger down the wallpaper, tracing its pattern. This was what she'd tried to avoid, all along. Being asked questions she didn't want to answer. Being quizzed. But . . . what was the alternative now? She wouldn't have come to Connie's if she'd been able to make sense of things on her own.

'It's . . . this person,' she said, jerkily. 'The one who's interfering with the game. He . . . knows things about me, things no one could know.'

'Like?'

'Like the nightmare I've had since I was a baby. And the private name my father calls me.'

Connie didn't look impressed. 'Loads of people must know those things. Your parents, for a start.'

'Not Laura,' Miriam said quickly. 'I made Dad promise he'd never tell her about my dream. No one knows about it. Except me and — ' She looked down at her fingers and began to talk even faster. 'Look, we don't need to go through all this. I've found out something peculiar about Christine and that boy. Why don't I just tell Hesketh tomorrow, when I go to K & K?'

'And?' Connie said.

'And . . . and he can sort it all out.'

'Great. Maybe you'll get a medal.' Connie snorted. 'That's all you want, is it? To stop some other company wrecking Hesketh's precious tests?'

Miriam ran her finger back up the wallpaper, but she didn't say anything. After a moment, Connie slid down on to the floor beside her.

'If I were in your place,' she said, softly, 'I wouldn't care much about K & K. But I *would* want to know who'd told my secrets. And why.'

135

'Would you?' Miriam said. Not looking up. 'Are you sure?'

'What's the alternative? You can't go on dodging the question for the rest of your life. And you're not going to forget about it, are you? *Why don't you ask your father if he did it?*'

'Oh, you think it's so easy, don't you!' Miriam buried her head in her hands. 'If you want to ask your dad something difficult, you've got this whole house. While your mum's in the kitchen, you can go upstairs, downstairs — anywhere. But it's not like that on the boat. It's impossible to have a private conversation. There's no *room*.'

Connie looked hard at her. 'It must be very difficult,' she said smoothly. 'I'm sure your dad understands that. I'm sure he would buy a proper house. If he had the money.'

Sharply, Miriam caught her breath. She lifted her head and glared. 'Don't you *dare*—'

But Connie was relentless. 'Take it out of the back of your head, Miriam. Look at it properly. You know your dad's short of money. You know he hates the way you quarrel, because you're so cooped up. So you're scared he's been got at, by someone who's trying to wreck these tests. You're scared he's sold your secrets. *Aren't you?*'

'Of course not! He wouldn't!'

'That's what I think!' Connie said, triumphantly. 'So it can't hurt to ask him, can it? You'll never stop fretting about it until you do. Why don't you come downstairs, now, and phone him up at work? No one will interrupt you here.'

'But ... won't your mum mind?'

'Why should she? Just go into the dining room and do it.'

Connie grasped Miriam's hand firmly and led her downstairs. Then she went into the kitchen, to talk to her mother. Miriam shut the dining room door and walked across to the telephone. As she looked up the number of the shop, her fingers were trembling. *Maybe he won't be there. Maybe they won't let me speak to him.*

But nobody seemed to mind at all. The moment she said his name, someone went off to call him to the phone and a second later, he was there.

'David Enderby. Can I help you?'

Miriam sat down with the phone in her lap. 'It's me, Dad.'

'Miriam?'

She could almost see his face. Mildly surprised, and half-smiling. Vulnerable. But it was too late to back out now. She plunged on, before he could ask what she wanted.

'You know those friends you were talking about yesterday? The computer people?'

'Yes?' He was cautious now. 'What about them?'

'I—'

'What's all this about, Minnow?'

Miriam could feel him drawing back. Suddenly, she realized how the phone call must seem to him. A way of shutting Laura out. Of asking something secretly, so that Laura couldn't overhear. She would have to come straight out with her question, now, otherwise he would slip away and evade it.

'There's something I need to know,' she said abruptly. She couldn't wrap it up, to protect him. Whatever words she used, he would know what she meant. 'Do any of those computer people know about my nightmare?'

There was a silence that seemed to go on for hours. 'That's a funny thing to ask,' her father said at last.

No. That was what she had expected him to say. *No, of course not.* Now that he hadn't, she was cringing inside, but she couldn't stop. She closed her eyes and screwed up her fists.

'Don't say anything else,' she muttered fiercely. 'I don't want to know anything else. OK? Just tell me that.'

137

There was thick darkness behind her eyelids. And, through the darkness, she could feel something coming towards her. But it couldn't be true. It *couldn't*.

Then her father laughed. His familiar light, apologetic laugh. 'Well, actually — yes,' he said. 'One of them does know.'

Miriam could hardly breathe. She growled down the phone, sounding even fiercer because she knew she couldn't bear it if he started explaining, or excusing himself. 'Who is it? Just the name.'

'Minnow — '

That was the last straw. '*Tell me!*'

As he said it, Connie's voice sounded, outside in the hall. That didn't stop Miriam from hearing, but she made her father say it again anyway. Just to be certain. Then she swallowed hard and spoke as fast as she could.

'OK. Now forget I even asked you. Don't say another word about it, ever again.'

'But, Minn — '

'Promise!'

He hesitated for a moment. Then he said, 'If I have to. I promise. But . . . are you sure you're all right?'

'I'm fine,' Miriam said shortly. 'But I think I'll stay at Connie Baxter's house tonight.'

'What shall I tell Laura?'

'Oh . . . tell her what you *like*! Tell her everything, if you want to!' Miriam slammed the phone down and buried her face in her hands.

After a moment, Connie tapped on the door and put her head round. 'Better?'

When Miriam didn't answer, she came right into the room and shut the door.

'What's the matter? Didn't you phone?'

'I phoned,' Miriam said. She lifted her head and looked up at Connie. 'Can I stay here tonight? Just until . . . until I get my head sorted out?'

'Of course you can,' Connie said. She hesitated. 'It's not really true, is it? He didn't tell?'

Miriam swallowed. It was an effort to get the words out. 'One of . . . his friends knows. So he must have done. He must have told — '

For a second, she couldn't say the name. Because it altered everything, shifting and rearranging it into quite a different pattern. A whole new world.

Connie looked shaken. 'I wouldn't have made you phone. Not if I'd thought it was true. Are you sure?'

'It *has* to be,' Miriam said harshly. 'How else would he know that Hesketh knows?'

'*Hesketh?*' Connie stared at her. 'But that's crazy. Why would he want to wreck his own tests?'

'I don't think he's trying to wreck the game,' Miriam said, unsteadily. 'It feels more as though he's trying — '

'As though he's trying to wreck you?'

Miriam rubbed her eyes. Even that didn't sound far-fetched now. She felt as though anything was possible, however unlikely and horrible it was. And she had a sudden hunger to talk to someone who knew what that meant. Who would understand how the world was coming apart and wouldn't expect her to make sense of it.

'I must get in touch with Stuart,' she muttered. 'He's got a right to know what's going on.'

Connie raised her eyebrows. 'How are you going to find him?'

'I'll have to go back into the game. Without telling Hesketh what I've found out.'

But that wasn't as easy as she thought it would be.

It was simple enough to invent an evil wizard called 'Hesketh' and plot to overthrow him. But when she came face to face with the real Hesketh, on Wednesday afternoon, everything shifted and dissolved again.

Because he hadn't changed. He was still massive and crumpled. The clever, comic, dangerous man who had said, *Just go with the game. And trust me.* It would have been so restful and pleasant and easy to throw away her suspicions and let him take over everything. She wished she could still do it. Trusting him felt right.

Like trusting her father.

The whole K & K building swam around her as they walked through it. The bricks and glass were no more solid than the cartoon walls of the New World dungeon, and Hesketh himself was shifting and changing as she looked, like one of the grey shapes from the game. He was an evil wizard now, but would he be transformed if she found a magic word? Would everything rearrange itself again, to uncover new dangers and different enemies?

She didn't dare try and speak, but Hesketh seemed to find her silence quite natural. He grinned when he left her at the test room door, throwing it open as though he were letting her into a wonderful, forbidden kingdom.

As he walked away, Miriam stared after him, wondering, for the first time, how he watched the game, and what shapes he saw. Then she shut herself in and went over to the Game Tower.

She'd missed the rainbow room altogether.

Stuart must have logged in first and dealt with the map, because when she clipped her helmet shut, she found herself standing outside in a pale dawn light. She was in the middle of a great crowd of people in white tunics. Glancing down, she saw that she was wearing a white tunic too and she guessed that her hair was straight and dark as well, bound round the forehead with a strip of cloth.

As she stepped forward, the crowd parted in front of her, forming an avenue. It was the only way she could go and after a moment she raised her arm and glided ahead, between the rows of silent people.

No one looked at her. They were staring forward, towards a high, stepped pyramid that towered above them all. In front of the pyramid stood a tall man in flowing robes, with a gigantic head-dress of coloured feathers. His face was stern and fierce, with a great hooked nose, like the beak of an eagle.

As Miriam drew close to him, she saw that her avenue was not the only one. Another avenue converged on it, from the right, and a line of boys was moving slowly to meet her. There were thirty or forty of them, all absolutely identical.

She glanced over her shoulder, guessing what she would see. Behind her stretched a line of identical girls. They were so like her that, as she looked back, so did they, each one turning her head with exactly the same movement.

Before she could work out what it meant, the two lines met in front of the pyramid. Miriam found herself standing next to the leading boy and, as she glanced sideways at him, his head turned too.

'Stuart?'

In real life, they would have been looking at each other, but this was not real life, and his eyes were focused somewhere beyond her face. He looked like a sleepwalker, and she hesitated for a moment, wondering whether she was wrong. Why should this boy, rather than one of the others, be the real Stuart?

In that moment, the tall man in front of them moved like lightning. His eyes flashed, horribly, and he raised his hand, flourishing something high in the air. Miriam saw its black shape clear against the pale blue of the sky, a wide blade, curved on both sides. Then he opened his mouth and yelled a single word, in a voice like a trumpet.

Viracocha!

In the same breath, the blade flashed down at the boy next to Miriam. It sliced straight through his white tunic, opening a wide, scarlet wound. Pushing his hand into the centre of the wound, the tall man pulled out something red and dripping, and held it high.

Miriam had time to think, *But that's disgusting! It's his heart, and it's still beating!* Then there was another yell, and

141

she saw the black knife flashing again, towards her own body.

She jumped back, but the body in the white tunic didn't obey her. In the game, she was paralysed, watching the knife dive towards her heart. The blood spurted scarlet, staining her tunic, and the priest flourished his hand high. Miriam waited for the end of the scene and the stone letters announcing her death.

But they didn't come. Instead, her viewpoint shifted, with a jump. Suddenly, she was further back, looking down at two bodies being dragged away. A boy's body and a girl's body.

Hers and Stuart's? She blinked and looked sideways.

It was like a repeat of that earlier moment. The new boy next to her looked sideways too, and their eyes didn't quite meet.

'Stuart?' she said.

Viracocha!

And the knife flashed for a third time, down towards the boy. Towards Stuart.

He hadn't spoken to her. Maybe he couldn't even hear her voice. But Miriam knew, without a doubt, that he was all the boys—just as she was all the girls. Waiting to be killed over and over again, in this repulsive ritual.

Chapter 23

Will let go of the mouse and stared at the horrible, casual carnage on the screen. He felt sick.

There was blood everywhere. Not real, tragic blood, but dramatic, spurting fountains of it, fanning out in decorative shapes as each sprite bit the dust. Pretty scarlet arabesques.

One by one, the bodies were dragged carelessly away and the hearts stacked on the altar at the top of the pyramid. One by one, the victims stepped forward, waiting meekly while the tall priest raised his hand.

There was nothing restrained or realistic about that priest. He was a towering monster, with a twisted, evil face and terrifying eyes that lit up as he sliced down with his black knife. In any other game, at any other time, Will would have enjoyed him utterly. He would have been working out how to use him better, to score more points.

But, this time, his mind kept filling in the details.

Each time one of the girls stepped forward, meek and docile in her white tunic, he saw that other girl from yesterday, with her quick movements and her sharp, living face. He felt her tug at his hands and heard her yell.

Let go! I haven't done anything! Let go!

And then each time, as the knife sliced and the body slumped, a boy came forward. And he knew who that boy was.

What was the point in pretending to himself? There might be straight hair and a white tunic in the picture, but in real life that boy had glasses and an Asher's College tie. And the sort of scrawny, nervous face that asked for trouble. Will had seen him pushed and hassled a dozen times. In the cloakroom. Behind the bicycle sheds. On the way home from school. *What's up, Jojo? Oh dear, your bag's gone in the mud. Have to be more careful next time, won't you?*

And he'd heard him yell back, miserable and desperate. *Push off! Why d'you keep picking on me?*

The knife sliced again, into the chest of the cartoon boy, and suddenly Will couldn't stand it any more. He reached forward abruptly and switched off. It was only a game, for heaven's sake! Why was he getting so worked up?

Because...

Because there were real people in that game. Somehow. Somewhere. Not being stabbed and sacrificed, but being tormented in some other way. He'd tried to ignore it, ever since Monday afternoon, but now their voices wailed inescapably in his ears.

... pathetic, hateful, unfeeling toad! If I ever get hold of you ... I trusted you, and you've spat it straight back in my face ...

That wasn't just simple fun. Not *playing*. And it wasn't acting either, because he'd seen Jojo on a stage, and it had been wooden and embarrassing. This stuff was real. And he couldn't go on with the game until he knew what it meant.

And who was in control.

He'd been pushing that question to the back of his mind, but it wouldn't go away any more. Standing up, he went over to the wardrobe and rummaged along the hangers, looking for the jeans he'd been wearing on Monday evening. When he found them, he slid his fingers into the pocket. The piece of paper was still there.

He didn't really need to read it again. He knew what the cutting was about, and the memo was plain enough. But he stared at the words, trying to convince himself that he'd misunderstood. Trying to force them into some other meaning.

They stayed obstinately plain and disturbing.

This scare could cost us millions, if we don't zap it before we bring the game out.
Time for a few experiments with fear, I think.

His father hadn't tipped him into some random, unknown game. Whatever this was, it was part and parcel of his own work. Part of those *experiments with fear.* His father was right in the middle of this whole, tawdry mess.

For ten or fifteen minutes, Will sat quite silent, trying to invent some other explanation for the things he knew. But nothing worked. Whatever had caused those taped shouts, they were real and ugly.

As ugly as the game.

Staring down at the paper, he remembered all its crude details. The racist stereotypes. The careless, cartoon violence. The murderous rats and comic kangaroos. It was a barren world full of cardboard figures, where nothing was certain except conflict and enemies and suspicion.

His father's world?

His?

He closed his eyes and thought about the spiders in the jungle. And the eyes in the temple. They had been small things at first, but he'd developed them as hard as he could. He had watched the sprites, second by second, working out what would scare them even more. Enjoying his own skill.

Was that how his father had felt, when he set the whole thing up?

Will went to find the telephone directory. It didn't take him long to track down the right number, because he knew what he was looking for. Sitting on his father's bed, he punched the buttons, with the phone cradled in his lap.

'Hallo,' he said. 'Mrs Jones? This is Will Barrington, from Asher's College. Can I speak to Stuart, please?'

Chapter 24

Miriam looked up at the knife again. There was no escape. She couldn't move backwards, or push through the people on either side. The only way that the game would let her move was forwards, towards the knife. She was a human sacrifice, and she didn't know what she was looking for, or what she could do.

Except die.

But she was still determined to get in touch with Stuart. If he didn't react to her voice, she would have to *do* something. Something clear and unmistakable that would show him she was on his side.

The knife dived down towards her, the blood spurted, and she saw her heart waved above her head, for the fourth time. Then she was jerked backwards again, becoming the next girl in line.

For the fifth time, she glanced sideways at Stuart. Now it was his turn to die, and he was trapped like her. Waiting for the inevitable death. Unable to move, except towards the knife.

The demonic face above them twisted venomously— and in that instant, staring up, Miriam realized what she had to do. She couldn't run back, to save herself, but she could run forward, to save Stuart. Without hesitating, she dived in front of him, flinging herself straight into the path of the knife.

The split second lag placed her underneath the blade as it came down, and she reached out both hands and grabbed it, trying to pull it away from Stuart and into her own body.

She didn't expect to survive. She didn't want to survive. As she leaped, she was braced for the spurting of her own blood, and maybe even the stone death-message on the

146

blanked-out screen. That was the *point*. She wanted to give up her own chance, to get her message across to Stuart.

But as her hands closed round the black knife, there was a burst of glorious, golden light. Behind the pyramid, the sun rose, brilliant and splendid, and the sky exploded into triumphant music.

WELL DONE, MIRIAM!
2000 POINTS!

In her hands was the murderous, jet-black blade. The treasure they must have come to find. And beside her was Stuart, his face turned away as he listened to the fanfare that meant she'd won again. Snatching the prize from right in front of him.

Staggering forward, carried by the force of her leap, Miriam yelled out despairingly. 'Stuart! I didn't mean it! I didn't want that to happen!'

But she knew it was no use. Maybe he couldn't even hear her. She hit the ground and rolled over, flinging the knife away in disgust, and it vanished as soon as it left her hand.

She was lying on her own, blindfolded and furious on the carpet of the test room.

The only thing that pulled her to her feet was the thought of Hesketh. She didn't know how much he had heard, or guessed, but she wasn't going to give away any more. Scrambling up, she began to take off her kit.

When Hesketh opened the door, he looked down at her curiously. 'You surprised me there,' he murmured. 'I didn't think you'd puzzle *that* one out in a hurry.'

Miriam tossed her head. 'Maybe I'm cleverer than you think I am.'

'Maybe you are,' he said. His voice was thoughtful.

'That was South America, wasn't it?' Miriam said quickly, to distract him. 'So we've visited all the continents. Is that the end?'

'The *end?*' Hesketh looked at her as though he couldn't believe what she had said. Then he threw back his head and bellowed with laughter, in a great, mocking shout that shook his whole body.

Last time, that huge laugh had mesmerized Miriam, pulling her into his enchanted world. Sucking the savour out of everything else and leaving her desperate for the game. But this time she felt quite detached. Coolly, she watched his vast, shaking shoulders and the gold of his earring and his teeth.

'What's left then?' she said.

He put a heavy arm round her shoulders and squeezed them. 'You haven't found the Rainbow Crystal yet. Next time, I'll give you all the treasures — whether you found them or not — and you can race Stuart to the Crystal and the real New World. That's the best bit, Minnow, believe me.'

Minnow. The moment he'd said it, Miriam felt him realize the mistake. He laughed again, but this time the laugh was forced, and his arm tightened, almost imperceptibly, around her shoulders.

At any other time, she would have given herself away. With a flicker of the eyes, or a tightening of the mouth, she would have let him see that she'd noticed. But she'd come straight from the game, and she was still in battle alert, with her pulse thudding and her reactions knife-sharp. Without hesitating, she grinned up at him, her eyes gleaming.

'Do we *have* to wait until Friday? Can't we have another session tomorrow?'

It worked. He relaxed, squeezing her shoulders again. 'I don't see why not. If Stuart can do it. Come tomorrow unless I get in touch.'

Miriam ducked away, grinning, and slid the last bracelet into the case, as though she hadn't a care in the world.

But it was hard to keep up. When she left Hesketh, at the door of the building, she was utterly exhausted, drained by the effort of concentrating. She dragged down the road so slowly that she missed her bus and, when she climbed on to the next one, she was shaking with weariness.

By the time she reached the river, all she wanted was to go to bed. She trailed down the towpath, working out how little homework she could get away with, and limped over the plank on to the back deck.

But before she could sneak into her cabin, Laura was there.

'Miriam?'

'I'm sorry I'm late,' Miriam muttered. 'I'm dead tired. Maybe I'll just go and lie down.'

There was a split second when they stared at each other. Wearily, Miriam remembered that she hadn't been home the night before, and she braced herself for an inquisition.

But the question, when it came, was quite different from what she expected. Laura gazed shrewdly at her.

'You do look shattered. Do you want me to get rid of your visitors.'

'*Visitors?*' Miriam blinked. 'Who are they?'

A strange expression crossed Laura's face. Almost like amusement. 'I didn't quiz them. I'm trying to reform my wicked ways—or hadn't you noticed? They said you'd be expecting them, so I sent them into your cabin.'

'They said what?'

The world spun crazily inside Miriam's head. Anything seemed possible. Hesketh and Christine Riley could have been in there, sitting side by side on her bunk. Or a crowd of sinister K & K secret police, complete with truncheons and black leather uniforms. Or even those computer people, from her father's old cricket club, with their bottles of beer and their sneering faces.

'I can turf them out,' Laura said carefully. 'If you don't want to be bothered.'

Miriam was so exhausted that, for a moment, it seemed like a wonderful offer. All she had to do was nod, and Heroic Laura would charge in and drive out the mysterious visitors. Laura would protect her, so that she could fall into her bunk and go to sleep. If only...

But she couldn't nod. She needed to know what was going on.

'It's all right, thanks,' she said. She met Laura's eyes and smiled. It wasn't a very energetic smile, but it meant —more than she could work out. 'I'll be fine.'

She stepped through and pushed the cabin door open. And there they were, standing in the middle of the cabin. Stuart and the freckle-faced boy from Beauchamp Terrace. Together.

'Don't be frightened,' the boy said quickly. 'There's been enough of that.'

Miriam's eyes flicked from his face to Stuart's and back again. Panicking. *They're all in it.* The boy was linked with Christine. Who worked for Hesketh. Who had heard about the nightmare from her father. And now Stuart, the one person she'd thought she could trust, had turned up with the boy.

There was nowhere to go. No way out.

She sat down hard on the edge of her bunk.

'What do *you* know about it?' she muttered. 'What's it got to do with you?'

The boy was very pale, but he looked at her steadily. 'I know that Hesketh's been trying to frighten you. Experimenting with fear. And he's got to be stopped. That's why I made Stuart come and see you.'

Stuart's mouth tightened. 'I told you,' he said to the boy. 'It's no use talking to her. She doesn't care.'

He wasn't even looking at Miriam. When she glanced down, she saw his hands, screwed into fists, and she knew that it wouldn't take much to make him run away. A few hard words. A little sneer. She could be rid of him whenever she liked.

150

The other boy was different. He was tense too, but he was staring straight into her eyes, challenging her, and he might not be so easy to fend off. But she could try.

And then the boy spoke. His voice shook slightly, but it was clear and determined. 'When you saw me in the flat, I'd just found out . . . that you were real people. If I'd known, I would never — ' He dropped his eyes. 'Hesketh wanted someone to watch your reactions and frighten you as much as possible. Someone who would enjoy torturing his enemies. So he chose me.'

Stuart said, 'You're not being fair to yourself, Will. You *didn't* know.'

'You think that makes it better?' Will said roughly. 'He's used me — just like he used you.'

Miriam could feel the misery. All she wanted was to be rid of them both, to chase them away and forget about the game. But there was no hope of forgetting, and if she missed this chance to understand what was going on, there might never be another one. She was in the middle of the whole wretched tangle, with no way to go except forward.

And the only way forward was to open up.

Staring down at the worn threads of the carpet, she made herself speak. 'He used me too. Those eyes in the dark — I wasn't telling the truth. They've been my nightmare, ever since I was little. And Hesketh *knew.* He used them to frighten me.'

She was watching Stuart, but it was Will's face that changed. It twisted wretchedly, and he sat down opposite, on Rachel's bunk.

'What are we going to do?' he said.

Miriam took a deep breath. 'First of all, I need to know what's going on. *Why* did Hesketh pick us out like that?'

'Because he knew how to frighten us.' It was Stuart who answered. 'If K & K want to sell New World, they've got to prove it doesn't scare children silly. Hesketh must have invented a cut-out that shuts the game down if people get too terrified.'

151

'So when you saw the spiders, and when those eyes came at me —'

'That's right. My heart began thudding away and suddenly the whole thing switched off — zap!' Stuart struck his hand against the bunk. 'I hadn't got a clue who'd done it.'

'But you'd done it yourself, without knowing.' Will looked up. 'That's the only thing that makes sense, isn't it? I bet the cut-out's tuned to a particular pulse rate. If it picks that up, you're out of the game. It's probably quite a simple device.'

'In the glove,' Miriam said slowly. She remembered the thick wristband, and the way Hesketh kept reminding her to keep it next to her skin. 'It has to be there. But I don't see — why go to all that trouble? Why not just make games that don't frighten anyone?'

'You *know* why.' Stuart's voice was harsh and angry. 'It has to be frightening, *because that's what people want.* You didn't keep coming back because the game was safe and pretty, did you? You came back because the danger speeded up your pulse and made you excited. It gave you a high, and you wanted that again. So did I. And part of me still wants it.'

His voice sharpened and stopped, and Will shook his head gently.

'You couldn't help it. It's the endorphins, and the adrenalin in your bloodstream. Anyone would have got hooked. That's why we've got to stop the game.'

Stuart's shoulders sagged. 'But it's too late, isn't it? K & K have got what they wanted. The glove works, and they can put the game on the market whenever they like.'

'We mustn't let them,' Will said stubbornly. 'It's an evil game. It's going to damage people.'

Miriam frowned. 'But the glove —'

Will waved his hand impatiently. 'They'll still get hooked. And anyway, you know the glove won't really work. Not in real life. People will just find out how to get round it.'

'Well, why don't we *tell* Hesketh that?'

'You think he'd care?' Will looked straight at Miriam, and his eyes were utterly bleak. 'He's got his tests, and they *prove* the glove's all right.'

'But—'

And then Miriam saw what they could do. The idea opened suddenly in her mind, as beautiful and simple as a rose and as terrifying as fire. She looked up at the two boys. At spindly, frightened Stuart, with his pop-eyes and glasses, and Will, with his bitter, miserable eyes.

'I know how we can wreck the tests and stop Hesketh,' she said. 'It's simple. We can do it tomorrow—if we dare.'

K & K: ELECTRONIC MEMO
JOHN SHELLEY TO HESKETH BARRINGTON
PRIORITY: URGENT

I've squeezed one more session for you. After that,
there's nothing more I can do. And I'd be glad to have
an assurance that you expect that session to be OK.

Just between ourselves.

K & K: ELECTRONIC MEMO
HESKETH BARRINGTON TO JOHN SHELLEY
PRIORITY: NORMAL

OK. Just between ourselves — it's great. Once New
World is set up with the Glove, we'll be able to milk the
game trauma scare for all it's worth. None of the
competitors will have an answer.

The Glove looks foolproof — but keep that to yourself.
I need the last session to tie up a few loose ends.

Chapter 25

Will spent the whole night thinking, *I can't do it.* Lying awake and staring at the ceiling.

His father was fast asleep across the lobby, and part of him wanted to run across, like a little child, and shake at that huge, sleeping shoulder. To yell, *You've got to stop it! I don't like it. Please make it stop!* As though the whole thing were some kind of bad dream that could be chased away.

That was how it had been when he was little. He would wake up, screaming his head off, and his father would be there, instantly. Always his father, even when his mother was still around. He'd scoop him up in a blanket, and sit him on his knee.

Right. Tell me all about your nasty dream. Then you can go back to sleep. It had always worked. Always.

But now there weren't any more bad dreams. At least, not when he was asleep. Instead, there was the nightmare game. And the job his father would lose if it didn't come right.

But it mustn't come right.

Will didn't waver in that, all through the long terrible night. Or even in the morning, at breakfast. He kept his determination and his secret, and he managed to sit opposite his father and mutter about the news, as usual, even though the world was coming to an end. But part of his mind was hoping that Miriam's plan would turn out to be impossible.

When Christine came in at twenty-past four, in a hurry as usual, he watched her fingers rattle over the keyboard and longed for her to look up and shake her head. *Sorry. Can't get in today. Someone must have found out what we're up to.*

But that didn't happen. It couldn't happen, because she wasn't really hacking. Now that he knew, he could see that

155

she was simply logging in, inputting a long sequence of passwords.

And there was the octagonal room. With a grin, Christine stood up and waved her hand, and Will sat down heavily, staring at the pile of treasures beside the glass case. At the rope and the wheel and the swords, the knife from South America and a leather pouch that must have been hidden among the kangaroos. At least there were no spiders yet. And no bright little eyes.

Christine must have noticed something odd about him. She usually raced off, the moment she'd set him up, but this time she stopped, with her hand on the door handle.

'Is everything OK?'

'Of course it is.' Will made himself grin. 'It's fine. This looks like the end of the game, doesn't it?'

'Could be,' Christine said, airily. 'How's it coming along? Got any idea of how it works yet?'

Gradually, Will let his grin fade. 'I *shall*,' he said, earnestly. 'I know I can do it, if I just get a few more chances to play.'

'I don't suppose there'll be many more,' Christine said lightly. 'Let's hope you're lucky today.'

Did she look relieved? Will couldn't tell. The next moment she'd gone, as usual, but this time he knew she wasn't hurrying back to K & K, to get on with her work. She was off to take the New World kit to Stuart's house.

He stared at the screen, waiting for the other two to log in. He couldn't tell which of them was first, because they were identical, but within a few minutes they were both there, squeaking away as they worked out what to do. For once, Will wished they would go on squeaking for ever.

But they didn't. With a nod, one of the sprites began to push the rope and the weapons into the leather bag while the other one glided over to the broken glass case, and the map.

Two grey hands hovered over the coloured continents. Every now and again, one of the sprites patted a patch of

156

colour, but all that appeared was a picture of one of the treasures. They'd visited all seven continents, and now they didn't know what to do.

But Will did.

He'd guessed already, out of the experience of hundreds of games. And because he knew how his father's mind worked.

But he didn't want to do anything about it. *I haven't got to. If they can't find out, they'll just waste this session, and no one will know I could have helped them.*

But that wouldn't do. He'd promised to play the torturer today. If he didn't, he would be letting the other two down. Unhappily, he picked up the mouse and slid his arrow across the map to the Atlantic Ocean in the centre. The place where the legendary eighth continent had sunk underneath the water. *Click.*

As the room started to spin, one of the sprites curled its hand for a second, giving him the thumbs up sign. Miriam, he guessed. He wished he hadn't known, because that made it easier for him to target her.

Resting his chin on his hands, he waited for the spinning to stop. When it did, there was a rustling, rushing noise and the last door swung open. The white door that led to the lost continent of Atlantis.

Beyond it, there was nothing but water. The grey Atlantic stretched endlessly in front of the sprites. Far away, on the horizon, a whale spouted and a school of dolphins jumped out of the water, the sunlight flashing off their curved backs, but there wasn't a centimetre of solid land to set foot in.

This time, Miriam was quicker than Will. While he was still wondering what they could do, she tapped Stuart on the shoulder and waved the prayer wheel at him. Then she glided up to the door and dropped it through, on to the surface of the water. It floated, bobbing at her feet, and she pointed down at it and squeaked to Stuart.

Surely they couldn't both fit on to that?

157

They didn't hesitate. At the same moment, they stepped forward through the door on to the wheel, balancing side by side. The door swung shut and there was nothing for Will to see, except the two of them on the wheel, and the unending water.

This time, they hadn't changed at all. They were both plain grey sprites, adrift on a grey sea. But on Will's screen something else changed dramatically. Suddenly a box appeared, all down the right hand side, filled with a scatter of coloured icons.

Spiders. Snakes. Dragons and serpents and monsters of all kinds. And, lower down, little scarlet flames and dark gaping boxes with lids that could snap shut to trap a sprite inside.

Will didn't need to scroll down to know that there would be eyes somewhere, as well. He was being offered every terror that could be put on the screen. An armoury of weapons to use against the sprites in this last level. If he hadn't known what was really going on, he would have been laughing with glee.

As it was, his arrow hovered for a moment over a safe, snarling dragon. But then he looked at the two sprites — at Miriam and Stuart, standing very tense and straight on the wheel — and he knew that he had to be as obstinate and tough as they were.

He had to torture them, as hard as he could.

He moved his arrow up to the spider and screwed his hand up for a moment, flexing the fingers. Then he clicked. And the spider went flying across the screen, straight towards the floating wheel.

Chapter 26

Miriam thought she was ready. Her whole body was braced against terror, ready for whatever Will could find to do to her. But the first giant spider took her by surprise, and she caught her breath.

It was vast. It came billowing across the water towards them, waving its huge jointed legs and swaying its monstrous abdomen. And she thought, *Stuart won't be able to bear it. He'll go mad.*

'Don't look!' she hissed. 'Close your eyes.'

Stuart's voice shook, but it was quite determined. 'Don't be silly. You know I've *got* to go on looking. I —'

And then he couldn't talk any more. She heard the words stick in his throat and she wished, desperately, that they hadn't started out. Why had she ever dreamed up this horrible, dangerous plan? It was all right to play with her own fears, but Stuart's were different.

As the second spider let itself down from the clouds, on a rope of gossamer as thick as a telephone wire, Stuart's right hand shot out suddenly and grabbed at hers. For a moment, in spite of everything, she nearly pulled away, drawing back into her own space. Then the pads inside her Game Glove inflated, and she realized what he'd done.

They were miles apart, in different buildings, on opposite sides of town. But she could feel the pressure of his fingers, across all that space. It was a secret signal that Hesketh couldn't monitor, whatever equipment he had. Because he couldn't know what it meant.

Miriam squeezed the fingers, reassuringly, and after a second's lag she felt Stuart squeeze back, in reply. Tightening her hand, she stared straight ahead, at the spiders, trying to share Stuart's terror. To make it more bearable by the steadiness of her hand.

159

Neither of them made any attempt to pull out the weapons or attack the spiders. They just stood on the wheel, floating across the ocean. Waiting for the moment when the huge creatures stopped dropping from the sky.

When they did, Miriam was taken by surprise. She had been so aware of Stuart's terror, of the stiffness of his body and the quick, shallow sound of his breathing, that she hadn't given a thought to what was coming next. All of a sudden, the horizon tilted, and the water came rushing up towards her. She tried to redress the balance, leaning sideways and pulling at Stuart's hand.

'Don't,' he said. She could hear how the strain of speaking dragged at his throat. 'We're going down ... into ... the dark.'

The warning was only just in time. Almost before he had finished speaking, there was a rush of water round her face. Bubbles exploded, splashing round her ears, and they sank into a fading green twilight that scrolled up in front of them.

Down into the dark.

Miriam knew what to expect. She even thought she was prepared. But when the light died, and the first bright dots pricked out the darkness, she clutched hard at the hand she couldn't even see.

'Don't—' For a second she felt, ridiculously, that she would drown if she opened her mouth. But she had to get the words out, before it was too late to speak. 'Don't take any notice if ... if I scream.'

The answer was a quick squeeze of her fingers. Then the whispers rustled up, drowning the vibrations of her voice.

... *min-now, min-now, min-now* ...

Darkness swept towards her, into the very centre of her head, and the eyes blinked closer and closer, their horror mixing with the worse horror in her mind. In her imagination, she saw her father leaning close to Hesketh. Grinning apologetically as he whispered in his ear. Telling him—

I can't scream. I can't!

The only fixed thing in the world seemed to be Stuart's hand, clenched steady and tight round her fingers. She clutched at it and, even though it was pitch dark and she couldn't see anything, she turned towards his face. Towards where his face ought to have been.

And a pair of eyes—too close, impossibly close—gleamed at her through the darkness.

Then she did scream. Helplessly, as though her whole life were pouring out of her, she opened her mouth and yelled and yelled and yelled—

It was like the nightmare. It was worse than the nightmare had ever been since she was very small. She was way back in the days when she was four or five, screaming without control because there was nothing she could do, herself, to shut off the terror. Because someone else would have to come, from outside, and pull her out. Someone would have to—

The hands closed round her. Huge hands, as though she were still a little child. They ripped at the wristband of the glove, diving underneath it to find the strip of plastic wrapped round her arm. The plastic that masked the beating of her pulse.

'You fool! You stupid, destructive, *suicidal* little fool!'

Hesketh's voice was angrier than any voice she had ever heard in her life. For a second, while she could still see the pictures of the game, everything came together. His voice, and the eyes in the dark, and the steady, reliable pressure of Stuart's hand.

Then the Game Glove picked up the desperate racing of her pulse and suddenly the whole thing cut out. Eyes, hand—everything. There was only Hesketh, tugging off her glove and hauling at the straps of her helmet.

She was rigid and paralysed, as though the nightmare had come in her sleep and she had just woken up. But instead of the lapping sound of the water, all she could hear was the steady sound of Hesketh swearing in her ear.

Then he wrenched the helmet off, and she saw his face, blazing down at her. He was as terrible as thunder. Gigantic and violent and very, very angry.

'What did you think you were doing? If you put that plastic in, you must have known — '

'Yes,' Miriam said. 'I knew.' It was still hard to speak, or even to breathe, but she had to keep going. 'The glove's supposed to take my pulse, isn't it? So it can stop me being too frightened.'

'That's right! So why on earth did you interfere with it? Did you *want* to be scared out of your wits?'

Miriam lifted her head defiantly. 'I'm not a baby. I can handle anything Stuart can. And when he said — '

They'd worked it all out, every word she was going to say, but she didn't have to finish. Hesketh grabbed her arm and she thought he was going to hit her.

'Stuart's done it as well?' he bellowed.

'He said I was scared. He said I wouldn't dare — '

'Did he?' Hesketh dragged at her arm. 'Let's talk to him.'

He tugged her out of the room and down the corridor. She found herself being pulled in at the door of the teleconference room where she had first seen Stuart. Hesketh pushed her into a chair and seized a telephone and she heard him growling into the receiver.

'Christine? What the hell's going on over there? No, don't try and tell me. I want to do it in teleconference. Face to face.'

He fumbled and jabbed at the keyboard, hissing at Miriam all the time.

'Do you know what you've thrown away? If you play the endgame properly, it doesn't cut out when you get too scared. It's the terrors that cut out. Then you find the Crystal, and — '

He strode down the room and pushed Miriam sideways to thrust his face in front of the screen.

'And?' Miriam said faintly.

Hesketh gave her a long, slanting look. 'And then you get to the New World,' he said softly. 'Atlantis rises from the sea, and you can do *anything*. You can rebuild reality however you want.'

His words washed round Miriam, but she couldn't answer. Swaying in her chair, she saw the screen begin to clear. Hesketh whipped round to face it. A boy stared out at them, stubborn and determined, with wretched eyes. He was very pale and panting slightly. *He must have run all the way*, Miriam thought.

It wasn't Stuart. It was Will.

Chapter 27

Hesketh caught at the edge of the table, and Miriam slid away out of her chair to let him sit down. He sank on to it without a sound, staring at the face on the screen.

'I worked it out,' Will said, in a tight, clipped voice. 'I told you I would.'

Hesketh's breath rasped in his throat. 'Where's Stuart? What's going on?'

'He cheated the glove,' Will said in the same relentless way. 'And everyone else will cheat it too, when the word gets around. It doesn't *work*.'

'Of course it works,' Hesketh said impatiently. 'The tests show — '

'The tests show the *truth*!' That was Miriam. She tugged at his sleeve, to make him hear her. 'And the truth is — no one's going to let you water the danger down. If you put it into the game, they'll find ways of getting round the cut-out. Whatever you do. They'll *dare* each other, and do it even if they're petrified.'

Will nodded. 'The glove's no good. You can't let them sell that game. It's dangerous.'

'You think I can stop them?' Hesketh said scornfully. 'They've sunk *millions* into it. They'll sell it now, whatever I do.'

'Not if you go to the papers,' Will said. 'And tell them the truth about today's test.'

'You think I'm going to wreck my own game?' Hesketh said. 'I've spent years on it, Will. It's not like anything else. Wait till you see the end, when the players walk on to Atlantis. It will transform the way people see the world — '

'You can't let them sell it,' Will said stubbornly. 'You've got to stop them.'

He was gazing at Hesketh, clutching with his eyes, the way Miriam had clutched Stuart's hand. And all of a

164

sudden, she understood who he was. It was so obvious that they hadn't even bothered to tell her.

Will was Hesketh's son.

Even now, he was hoping for miracles. Waiting for his father to brush all the troubles away. Miriam felt as though something sharp had twisted painfully in the centre of her chest. She pushed her face into camera shot.

'It's no good,' she said bitterly. 'Just because he's your father, it doesn't mean he's wonderful. I thought *my* father was like that. I thought I could trust him and he'd always look after me. But he told Hesketh about my night-mare — when he'd promised never to tell anyone. You're out on your own, Will.'

Will's face changed. She had hit him where he couldn't defend himself. In the soft, childish centre, where he still believed that his father could make everything all right.

His father, the wizard.

But it was no use. Miriam saw him begin to believe her. His angry, optimistic stubbornness faded and the light in his eyes began to die away. Drowning.

She couldn't tell what Hesketh saw, because his expression didn't alter a fraction, but suddenly he said, 'You're wrong, Miriam.'

'Wrong?' For a second, she didn't understand what he was talking about. But she could see how he was staring at Will, and she knew he was deadly serious.

'It wasn't your father,' he said.

She couldn't speak. Struck dumb, she stared at the great slab of his face, at the sad, sorcerer's eyes, and the long twist of his mouth.

'It wasn't your father,' Hesketh said again. 'He never told me.'

It was no good. She couldn't trust him. She *mustn't* trust him. He was the wizard, the shape-shifter.

'If he didn't tell you — who did?'

A faint half-smile flitted across Hesketh's face. 'Don't you remember that day when we all came round?'

165

Miriam stared at him, listening to the soft, spellbinding sound of his voice. *Don't trust*— But he was speaking steadily now, like someone lulling a child to sleep. And a slow curl of hope rose like smoke in her mind.

'We came when that stepmother of yours was off at a meeting. It was a sort of silly joke. A whole crowd of us dropped in for a drink one evening, just the way we used to. We knew your father wouldn't turn us out on his own, and I suppose we hoped for a really juicy bust-up when Laura got back. You were asleep upstairs.'

He paused and Miriam pulled up the next chair and let herself down into it.

'What happened?' she whispered. 'Did I have a nightmare?'

A small smile twisted the side of Hesketh's mouth. 'You had the mother and father of all nightmares. And poor old Dave hadn't got a clue what to do. So I pulled you out of his arms and wrapped you up in a blanket. And I said—'

But he didn't speak the words, because Will's voice came from the screen, speaking them for him. One by one, as though they hurt his mouth.

'You said, *Tell me all about your nasty dream*, didn't you? *Tell me all about your nasty dream. Then you can go back to sleep.*'

Miriam couldn't take her eyes off Hesketh. '*I* told you?'

Neither of them answered. They were staring at each other so hard that they might not even have heard her. But she knew the answer anyway. Slowly, she felt her mind relax, and she stood up.

'Thank you,' she said.

But she couldn't just go. Not like that. She looked at the taut, tense face in the screen. At the heavy fists, lying clenched on the table in front of her.

'It could all be all right,' she said softly. 'You could *make* it all right, Hesketh.'

For a second, she hunted for something else to say. But there wasn't anything else. The two of them were locked together by that steady, enchanted gaze. It was their story, not hers.

She slid out of the room and for the first — for the only time — she walked through the K & K building on her own, seeing it with her own eyes. It glittered around her like a great bubble, bright and magic and trivial. A place where you could remake the world, however you fancied. When she got to the front door, she let herself out without a backward glance and ran down the steps.

The telephone box was full, and three people were queuing. By the time her turn came, she'd had plenty of time to work out what she wanted to say.

'Connie?'

'Did it work?' Connie said anxiously. 'Are you all right?'

'Everything's fine,' Miriam said. 'I can't wait — ' Suddenly she realized it was true, and she grinned at her reflection in the window of the telephone box. A sharp, clever face, with very bright eyes. 'I can't wait to tell you all about it.'

Connie didn't need a screen to see the expression on that face. They'd known each other for a long time. 'You sound really pleased with yourself. In fact, you sound pleased with everything. When am I going to hear?'

'How about this evening? Can you come to the boat?'

There was a little pause. 'I thought it was impossible to be private there. What about Laura?'

In the window, Miriam's reflection grinned again. 'That's why we have to go to the boat. So I can explain to everyone at once.'

There was another, longer pause. Then Connie said, 'You *are* all right, aren't you? Now there's a surprise.'

The questions hovered somewhere in the air between them. Connie didn't speak them aloud, and no electronic bugging could have picked them up, but Miriam knew. It was part of their friendship. And she quite enjoyed the thought of deciding which questions to answer.

But all she said, for the time being, was, 'I'll be there in an hour or so. Could you go round and warn them I'm going to be a bit late? I've got to go down to the Centre on my way home.'

K & K: ELECTRONIC MEMO
HESKETH BARRINGTON TO JOHN SHELLEY
PRIORITY: NOW

We've hit an unforeseen problem. Do nothing,
REPEAT NOTHING until we speak.

I hope you listened to my advice about waiting,
Shelley, otherwise you're going to be SICK.

Chapter 28

Miriam had picked the Centre yesterday, because it was neutral. Away from everyone's home. Now, as she walked into the bright, busy shopping mall, she saw what she'd done. It was crowded with girls she knew, and boys in Asher's College blazers. She hesitated half-way down the first avenue, looking round warily.

'Hey!' said a voice on her right. A surprised, delighted voice. 'You've jacked in the computer course after all, have you?'

It was Debbie, hanging on the arm of a tall boy with his red hair cut very short. She was grinning all over her face.

'Yes,' Miriam said. 'I won't be going there any more.'

'But that's great! You can come and meet everyone. Pete, this is my friend Miriam — '

Pete smiled too. He was very tall and good-looking, in a brutal, self-assured way, and he looked ready to talk. But Miriam glanced past him, towards the fountain, and saw the figure standing there. Waiting for her.

Pete followed her eyes. 'Hey, look, Debs!' he said. 'Look who's crawled in off the street.' And he sniggered.

Debbie turned too, to stare down the mall. Stuart saw them watching him, and he shifted awkwardly, pretending not to notice. If Miriam hadn't known, she would have put him down as smug and superior. The kind of boy who always tried too hard and stood too close.

But she was used to guessing his feelings now, from the way he stood, and she could tell that he was struggling not to run away. She could ignore him if she wanted to, and join in with Debbie's giggling. He wouldn't come down to meet her.

She could ignore him — but he hadn't ignored her, in the nightmare under the water. She could still feel the steady grip of his hand.

She smiled at Debbie. 'Sorry, I can't hang around. I've come to meet someone.'

Even then, it wasn't easy. She walked down the mall, between the glittering glass shop fronts, feeling their eyes on her every inch of the way. Waiting to hear the sniggers start again, to include her. But she wasn't going to give up. *You can rebuild reality however you want to.*

It was true. She could. But no wizard could help her. There was no power in magic crystals or continents that rose from the sea. Reality was built out of small things, like holding a hand and keeping a promise. Without worrying who was watching.

'Hi, Stuart,' she called, as soon as she was near enough. 'Can we go back to the boat? I've got a lot to tell you, but I want my . . . parents to hear it too.'

He nodded and began to walk towards her. Then there was a shout from the other direction. Turning, Miriam saw a tall, dark-haired figure running down the opposite mall. It was Will, racing as though he had wings on his feet.

He was too far away for Miriam to see the expression on his face. She took a step closer, trying to work out how he felt from the way he moved, but it was no use. She didn't know him well enough yet.

So she stood patiently, waiting for them both with the firm ground under her feet. Watching their reflections glitter along the lighted shopfronts, flickering and changing as they came.